NIKOLAI
my love

To Rose,
a wonderful friend
and relative. Enjoy the
book.
Love,
Mary Ann

Maryl Damian

ISBN: 1523377275
ISBN 13: 9781523377275
Library of Congress Control Number: 2016901846
CreateSpace Independent Publishing Platform
North Charleston, South Carolina

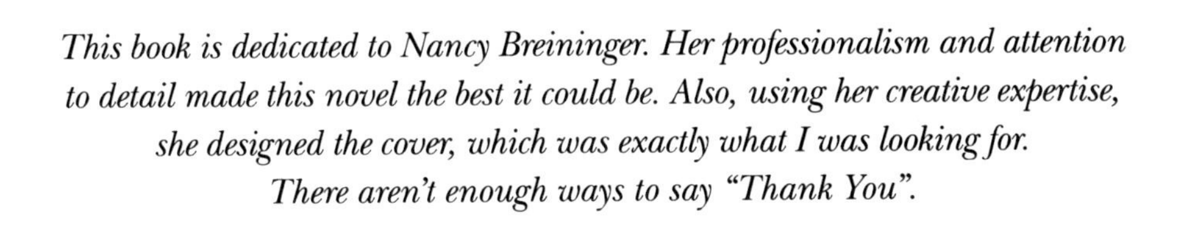

This book is dedicated to Nancy Breininger. Her professionalism and attention to detail made this novel the best it could be. Also, using her creative expertise, she designed the cover, which was exactly what I was looking for. There aren't enough ways to say "Thank You".

1

Leaning into the biting wind, Nikolai pulled up the collar of his wool coat and jammed his rough, chapped hands deeper into his pockets as he rounded the street corner leading to the alley. As he neared the door to his room at the back of the diner where he worked as a short order cook, the harsh scraping of metal against metal caught his attention. He halted in mid-step and scanned the trash barrels that lined the brick wall.

Suddenly, stacked garbage cans catapulted toward him, spewing an avalanche of slimy, rotted food on the ground in front of him. Whirling around to run, Nikolai felt a mind-numbing blow to the back of his head. As he dropped to his knees, he saw a fleeting figure in black dart into the shadows before unconsciousness claimed him.

He awoke a while later, face down in the dirt with a throbbing pain on the crown of his head. Gingerly, he touched the spot where a lump, crusted with blood, had formed. He spat out gritty granules of dirt as he slowly rose. Steadying himself against the wall, Nikolai fumbled in the pocket of his jeans for his key, and leaning heavily on the door, he pushed it open.

As he staggered into his cold, drafty room, he made his way to the cot against the wall, but before he lay down, a sobering thought came to him. Frantically, he checked his jacket pocket, moving his hand along the bottom of it to a hole which led into the lining. He swore.

The lining had been slit with a knife. The money hidden there was gone. Six hundred dollars—almost everything he had saved since he had come to this country.

Too cold to take off his jacket, he sank down on the cot and leaned back against the peeling plaster wall. As he pulled the old wool army blanket over him, someone knocked at the door. Nikolai stumbled to his feet and picked up a bat he kept near the cot. Then warily he moved toward the door calling, "Who is there?"

"Tania."

He unlocked it and let his cousin in. When the thin blonde woman saw the dried blood in his hair, she asked in a flood of Russian, "Nikolai, what has happened to you?"

"I was knocked unconscious and robbed."

"Where?"

"Here in the alley."

"Are you all right?" she asked, placing a hand on his shoulder.

"Yes, there's just a little blood."

"Let me look at it."

Nikolai sat on the cot and pulled a pack of cigarettes from his shirt pocket. He tapped one out and lit it. Then he leaned forward, resting his elbows on his knees.

Tania peered down at the wound. "Oh, Nikolai, this must be cleaned."

"There is alcohol and a cloth in a box under the sink."

She lifted the tattered gray material that formed a skirt around the sink and found the box. Pawing through it, she pulled out a clean cloth and a half-filled bottle of alcohol.

As she dabbed at the cut, she asked, "Did they take all of your money?"

"Yes," he said, wincing in pain.

"That is terrible. Do you have any idea who they were?"

"No, but there must have been two. I saw the one who knocked over the garbage cans, but not the one who hit me. I think they might have been Russian because they knew where to look for my money."

"What can you do?" she asked.

He clenched his jaw as she probed the wound for any remnants of dirt. "You know I can do nothing without documents. If I go to the police to report the crime, they will have me deported as soon as they find out that I am here illegally. And the same thing would happen if I went to the hospital to have my head stitched."

He threw his hands up. "So here I am bleeding and penniless, and soon I will be out of a job."

"When will the diner close permanently?"

"Very soon, and I have not been able to find other work. If only I had a green card, it would not be so difficult. Have you heard of anything through our Russian friends?"

"No, but I have asked my employer to see if any of her acquaintances need a handyman or gardener."

He shook his head and laughed derisively. "Look what has become of Nikolai Mendeleyev, the learned physics professor. I would have been better off to stay in Russia and do the government's bidding or go to the prison camps and die of the cough."

"Don't say such things, Nikolai. Right now, Sergei is in contact with someone about getting counterfeit documents."

"Oh, yes, driver's license . . . social security, but I will never be able to work in my profession again."

She sighed, hovering over his shoulder. "Things will get better."

After the wound had been dressed, Tania set a scarred pan with water on the hot plate. When it boiled, she added a teaspoon of instant coffee. She sat down next to him on the cot and handed him the steaming mug. "What will your mother do?"

Nikolai covered his eyes with his calloused hand. "She will have to manage until I can save some money to send her."

"This must be a difficult time for her."

"It is not a good time for any of us."

Tania put her hand on his shoulder. “Please do not lose hope. I must go now. I will be back tomorrow with any news I hear.”

He stood and walked her to the door, locking it behind her. Then, he lay down on the cot to sleep with the slow steady drip of the ancient sink as his lullaby.

Beth Winters sat in the rocking chair by the bed watching her mother sleep. As the older woman rolled to one side, her hipbone created a sharp angle under the sheet. Beth’s eyes brimmed with tears. How thin her mother had become from the cancer in just a few months.

Beth brushed her hair back off her face as she studied the delicate birch leaves quivering in the November wind outside the window. What was she going to do? She needed more help taking care of her mother. She stood and gently pulled the blanket up over the shoulders of the sleeping figure.

In the kitchen, Beth stirred a pot of soup as she pondered the situation. The back door opened, and her friend Doreen Johnson let herself in. “Hey, how’s it going?”

“I’ve been better.”

Doreen, dressed in jeans and a sweatshirt, perched on the edge of a kitchen chair and rested her elbows on the table. “Hmm, smells good. Is that your mother’s famous recipe for chicken soup?”

“Yeah, want some?” Beth asked, turning toward her friend. Since their days as schoolmates at St. Mary’s Parochial School, Doreen’s wide grin and bright blue eyes had never failed to lift Beth’s mood.

“No, I already ate.”

“How are Joe and the kids?”

“Everybody’s busy. Joe’s still working overtime at the shop, and the twins are playing travel soccer, so that keeps me hopping. Thank God I have my knitting to take along.”

As Beth poured two cups of coffee from an electric percolator, she studied her friend—the perfect wife and mother and a master knitter; just the daughter her own mother would have given anything for.

Doreen pulled her chair closer to the table and accepted the cup of coffee Beth offered. "How's your mother doing?"

Beth shook her head. "She's weaker than she was, and once the home health care worker leaves, she's alone until I get home from the university. I wish I could find someone to check in on her. And then, there's the yard work. The leaves have to be two feet deep."

Doreen pushed longer wisps of her blunt-cut, light brown hair behind her ears. "Actually, you need two people, but that can get to be very expensive."

Beth sat opposite her. "I realize that, but what can I do?"

Suddenly, Doreen brightened. "You know, my Russian cleaning woman just told me about her cousin who came to this county a few months ago. She says he's desperate for a job, and he's very trustworthy. The only problem is he can't speak English very well."

"He doesn't need to speak good English to help me with my mother and do some work around here."

"I think he's a handyman, and I guess he'll work for just about nothing as long as he's given a room he can sleep in. Maybe he can do both jobs for the price of one."

"Do you think he might be interested?" Beth asked, lifting her mug in both hands.

Doreen shrugged. "Why not?"

Beth chewed on her lip for a minute in concentrated thought. Then she replied, "Have your cleaning woman talk to her cousin, but tell her I need someone very soon."

Tania's husband, Sergei, remained in the car while she and Nikolai made their way up the flagstone walk to the large L-shaped brick house. Nikolai studied the brass numbers on the front door, checking them against the information written on the slip of paper he held in his hand. He smoothed his hair back and rang the doorbell.

With the first snowflakes of the season whirling around him and his breath forming white clouds in the frigid air, he prayed Beth Winters would hire him. The diner had closed permanently, and he feared unless he found a position, he would have to rely on the hospitality of relatives to keep a roof over his head.

Nikolai nervously rubbed his cold hands together as he and Tania waited. When the door swung open, a pretty blonde stood in the doorway. Although her appearance was petite and delicate, her manner seemed strictly businesslike. "You must be Tania and Nikolai," she said without smiling.

"Yes, we are here for the interview," Tania answered.

"I'm Beth Winters. Please come in."

The foyer was bright and spacious. The hardwood floors gleamed, reflecting light that came in through the leaded-glass sidelight windows and a thick oriental carpet covered the center of the floor.

With small brisk steps, she led the way across the foyer into the library. He and Tania followed passing two doors on the right. One led to a kitchen of rustic knotty pine and the other to a more formal dining room. To the left, an archway opened into a large comfortable living room with an overstuffed sofa and chairs.

"Please sit down," she instructed as she sat in the leather chair behind the mahogany desk.

Her glance appraised the pair and then settled on Nikolai. "Do you have references?"

"Only one," he said in a thick Russian accent as he pulled a sealed envelope from his pocket.

"Just the one?"

Nikolai nodded.

Beth looked over the letter from his previous employer, which described Nikolai as hardworking, honest, and polite. Then she glanced up at him. He was medium height with broad shoulders and appeared to be in his early forties. His hair was dark and wavy.

She studied his face. His eyebrows were a rich brown and thick, as were his lashes. He had a strong, smooth jawline and a straight nose that broadened slightly at the nostrils. A small closely cropped beard covered his chin and extended upward in two thin lines ending just below the corners of his mouth. His neatly trimmed mustache lined full lips.

As he sat in front of her, he seemed uncomfortable and stared down at his hands often. However, when he did look her in the eye, she found his eyes were a golden-green and had a translucent quality that seemed to draw her in as she studied them, trying to decide which color they really were.

Beth began, "Nikolai, Mrs. Johnson tells me you will work for seven dollars an hour as long as you have a room to stay in."

The muscles of Nikolai's jaw worked, and he hissed in Russian to his cousin, "What does this woman think—I am riffraff? She calls me by my first name but calls her friend Mrs. Johnson."

"Nikolai, it does not matter . . ." Tania began.

"Is there a problem?" Beth cut in stiffly.

"No, no problem. Please continue," the young woman answered in English.

Irritated, Beth shifted her glance to Nikolai. "The work will consist of jobs like taking screens down, raking leaves, and cleaning the basement. Also, you'll have to check on my mother while I'm at work, and you may have to help me with her at times. Are these things you are willing to do?"

He answered quietly, " I can do."

"Also, there will be absolutely no smoking on the premises." Her eyes settled on the outline of the pack of cigarettes in his shirt pocket.

The muscle in his jaw hardened as he muttered under his breath, "I do not think this woman will even let me breathe here."

Tania shot him a stifling glance.

Beth continued, "Well, I'll want to talk to your previous employer. Then perhaps we'll give you a try. I'll be in touch with you sometime tomorrow."

Nikolai and Tania rose to leave. He nodded to Beth and then looked down at the cap he held in both hands. He was the picture of humility, but for some reason, Beth didn't think he had a humble bone in his body.

2

Nikolai was studying the small sofa in Tania and Sergei's living room and wondering how he would be able to sleep on it when Tania burst into the room.

She clapped her hands happily and said in rapid fire Russian, "Nikolai, you got the job. Miss Winters talked to your old boss at the diner, and he said very good things about you. She just called and said you can move in today."

"Good. Now I will not disrupt your household."

"Don't say such things. You know you are always welcome here."

"I know, but life will be easier for all of us if I have my own place to stay."

After lunch, Nikolai arrived at the Winters' home with all of his possessions stuffed in the large duffle bag slung over his arm.

Beth ushered him into the house. "Come with me. I'll introduce you to my mother, and then I'll show you your bedroom and bath."

Leading the way down the long hall, she stopped and opened the first door on the left. They entered a cozy cream-colored room with pine Shaker-style furniture and a high-backed colonial recliner whose headrest and armrests were draped with old-fashioned cutwork doilies. Lace tie back curtains adorned the windows.

The only incongruous piece of furniture was the metal hospital bed. In the bed lay an elderly woman with neatly combed white hair and brilliant blue eyes. Thin features added to the aura of frailty, but her sweet smile lit up her face with a radiance that feigned health.

"Mom, this is Nikolai— the man I told you about. He's going to do odd jobs around the house, and he'll look in on you when I'm at school."

Looking kindly into his eyes, the older woman extended her hand to him. "I'm so pleased to meet you, Nikolai."

He took her hand in his and kissed the top of it as he said, "Lovely lady."

Beth pursed her lips and folding her arms across her chest, tapped her foot lightly on the floor.

Mrs. Winters smiled at him. "You don't look Russian to me. I expected you to be blonde and blue-eyed."

In his best English, he said, "Many countries belong to Soviet Union before. My city is St. Petersburg, but one grandmother come from Bukhara—many dark-haired people there."

"Bukhara—isn't that where the rugs come from?"

"It is so, Madam."

"They're so beautiful. I always wanted to buy one."

"This is also beautiful." Nikolai pointed to the elaborate crocheted edging on her pillowcase. He looked at Beth. "You do this, Miss?"

"Absolutely not. I don't have time for that kind of nonsense."

Mrs. Winters sighed. "I've made everything that's crocheted in this room, Nikolai, but as you can see, Beth doesn't appreciate the effort."

"I think they're pretty," Beth cut in, "but I feel bad that you couldn't have spent your time doing something more fulfilling."

"For me, it was fulfilling."

"And," Nikolai added, "these are treasure you can give to grandchildren."

"If I ever get any." Looking at her daughter, the older woman sighed again.

Beth pulled up the knitted afghan on her mother's bed and said, "Mom, you're not cold are you?"

"No, no, I'm fine."

"Well, you look tired. Why don't you take a nap before supper? I'll show Nikolai his room."

Back in the hallway, Beth opened the next door and motioned Nikolai in. "I'm sure you will find this comfortable. For today, just get settled. Tomorrow you'll start working. You may use the phone by the bed to make calls. Supper is at six o'clock."

The moment she departed, Nikolai shut the door and stretched out on the bed, reveling in the thickness of the blankets and coverlet. Then, he reached over and felt the radiator, taking in the warmth it exuded.

The walls were painted pale lavender with white trim around the doors and windows, and the draperies were made of lined white chintz. Obviously this room had been meant for a woman, but no matter, he would sleep in it like a king.

He rolled off the bed and walked into his private bath. Yellow and lavender tiles formed an intricate pattern that covered the walls. The shower was so big five other people could get in with him. Nikolai shook his head. *Bathrooms are one thing the Americans have gotten right.*

Lying back down on the bed, Nikolai rolled up in the covers and dozed off, sleeping the decadent sleep of a czar. He awoke abruptly at six o'clock. Quickly, he washed his face and combed his hair, trying to look as presentable as possible.

The dining room was fairly large and wallpapered in a blue and white pineapple design that had the flat look of stenciling. In the center of the room was a dark pine table and chairs. A matching hutch displayed antique blue and white dishes. On the walls hung paintings—one, a still life of a bowl of fruit and another, a scene of a hunting dog poised to flush some sort of fowl out of tall grass. One place was set at the table.

A door led into the kitchen. Nikolai approached it, almost running into Beth, who was on her way out, carrying a platter with steak and baked potatoes in one hand and a salad bowl in the other.

"I will help," he said in his limited English.

"Can you get the two extra dishes and silverware on the counter?" she asked.

"Yes."

She set the platter and salad on the table, and when he returned with the dishes, she filled them with food. "I'm making plates for my mother and myself. I usually eat with her in her room. You may eat here if you like or in your room."

"I will eat with mother also." Living alone in the back room of the diner had left him with a need for conversation.

"That's not necessary," Beth replied. "Suppertime is your own time."

"I want to eat with mother—unless you not want me to."

"No, no, come with me. My mother will be happy to have some conversation other than mine."

As Nikolai entered Mrs. Winters' room with his dish and silverware, she said, "How sweet of you to eat with us. I'm anxious to get to know more about you and your country."

Nikolai smiled as he placed his dish on a small table and sat in the chair next to it. Inside, he was regretting his decision to join them. He had not yet formalized in his mind the lies he would tell them. Since he could not answer any questions about himself truthfully, Nikolai decided he would tell Beth and her mother about the life of a young carpenter he had known. This man's life and familial background would now become Nikolai's.

In better times, the fellow had worked for Nikolai's mother, and as an adolescent, Nikolai had learned quite a bit about carpentry from him.

Mrs. Winters ate small mouthfuls of meat and potatoes that Beth had cut into tiny pieces for her. Putting her fork down, she leaned her head back against the hospital bed, which had been cranked up to a sitting position. "So, you come from St. Petersburg. It must be a beautiful city."

"Yes, it is—how do you say—Venice of the North." He finished the sentence with the aid of a small Russian-English pocket dictionary.

"And your parents?" asked Mrs. Winters.

"My father do carpentry work like me," Nikolai lied. At that moment, he remembered the terrible argument in which his scientist father insisted that Nikolai work for the government just as he had. It had not been long after that that his father died.

"How old is your father?" she asked, bringing him out of his reverie.

"My father not alive now."

"Oh, I'm so sorry. What about your mother?"

Nikolai thought about his mother. This once affluent woman was bedridden, and because of his unsanctioned flight from the country, she no longer received her dead husband's pension. Now, she waited anxiously for the money Nikolai would send her from his meager income.

Cutting into his baked potato, he answered, "My mother not well."

"When will you be able to visit her?" the older woman asked in a kindly voice.

"I cannot go back. I must work so my mother can live. No jobs in Russia."

Mrs. Winters rolled her head from side to side against her pillow. "What a shame. She must miss you terribly."

Nikolai shrugged. "This cannot be helped."

"Still, it's sad."

As he set his dictionary down on the small table next to him, Beth asked, "Are you finding English difficult?"

"Yes. I try to learn from dictionary, television, and from listening to words in songs."

"At the university where I teach they have classes in English for foreigners. Are you interested in taking a class?"

"I cannot pay."

"That's alright. The professor is a friend of mine. I'm sure she'll let you just sit in on the classes. I'll talk to her and see when you can start."

He nodded and said, "Thank you."

"Are you married?" Mrs. Winters asked.

"No," Nikolai answered.

Following up her first question with another, the older woman asked, "How old are you?"

"Forty-three." He held up four fingers and then three to make sure she understood his rough English pronunciation.

"Oh, five years older than Beth."

Nikolai turned toward Beth. "You are married, Miss?"

"No, she's not," her mother answered for her.

"Why no husband for such beautiful woman?"

"Because she's too damn fussy," said her mother in an exasperated tone.

"What is fussy?"

"You know," the older woman waved a weak hand. "This one is too short, that one is stupid, this one is domineering . . . and on and on."

"Why do you not like men?" Nikolai cocked his head to one side and knit his brows together.

"It's not that I don't like men. At this point in my life, my career comes first," Beth snapped, cutting the last of her steak.

"For a woman . . . marriage, husband, and children most important," he said, placing his silverware on his empty plate.

"That's exactly what I've been telling her," Mrs. Winters interjected, nodding her head.

Beth glared at Nikolai. "I'm not about to drop everything I've worked for so that some man can rule my life."

"And you think all men do this? Do you think man marries a woman only to rule her?"

"Okay," she said, jumping to her feet. "That's enough of this conversation. Mother, give me your dish. I'll take it into the kitchen." She pierced Nikolai with another glowering look. "Come with me. I'll show you what I want done in the yard tomorrow."

Carrying his dish, he followed her into the kitchen, positive he had made himself an enemy.

With jackets buttoned and collars upturned against the cold November evening, they went out to the wooden deck. On it was a patio set with a glass-topped table.

Nikolai surveyed the yard littered with leaves. It was bordered at the back by a tall stockade fence and on the sides by willowy evergreens. A circular mulched area with a variety of bird feeders occupied one part of the lawn near the garage.

Beth pointed toward the lawn furniture. "All this has to be washed down and put away, and the yard has to be raked."

Then she turned abruptly and walked back into the house. He followed submissively. In the kitchen, Beth washed the pans and stacked them on the dish drain. She rinsed the dishes and put them in the dishwasher. Nikolai found a dish towel and started drying the pans. He chided himself for speaking his mind with her.

If she was not happy with him, she could fire him at any moment and send him out into the cold night. He must watch his tongue, at least until he got the false documents he needed to find other employment.

Beth made coffee. They sat across the table from each other in icy silence as they drank it. Nikolai thought, *The atmosphere is colder in here than in Siberia.*

Stealing glances at her, he assessed this strong-willed woman. She was pretty with small finely carved features, delicate enough to be made of porcelain and marred only by the light freckles which dotted her nose. Her eyes were light blue-gray. Her soft ash blonde hair was gently piled onto her head and secured with combs.

He studied her as she got up to put her cup and saucer into the sink. Her body was slim with ample breasts and rounded hips. Nikolai wondered how such a delicate looking woman could be so formidable when she was angry.

He rose also. "Do you mind, Miss, if I borrow some books from library room?"

"Please do not call me *Miss*. You can call me Beth." Then, softening her tone, she said, "Show me which books interest you."

In the library, Nikolai studied the titles and selected four of *The Leatherstocking Tales* by James Fenimore Cooper. He had read *The Last of the Mohicans* as a student of sixteen and fell madly in love with America and its noble Indians. In those days, no matter what the cost, when Nikolai came across one of Cooper's novels translated into Russian, he would buy it.

"Is it all right I take these?" he asked humbly.

Beth glanced at the titles and raised her eyebrows. "You want these?"

Nikolai nodded.

Beth shrugged. "Take any books you want."

Holding the volumes in both hands, he said, "Thank you," and headed down the hall to his room.

Lying on his bed, he opened the novel *The Deerslayer* and tried to glean some meaning from the first few pages. He checked his pockets for his dictionary, but it seemed to be missing, so he abandoned the effort and decided to take a shower.

He swung his legs off the bed and removed his shoes and socks. In the bathroom, he unbuttoned his shirt and hung it on a hook.

Smoothing his hair back with his palm, he looked in the mirror. *What was it about him that so offended Beth?*

Nikolai finished undressing quickly and stepped into the shower. He manipulated the knobs until warm water streamed from the showerhead. For five full minutes, he reveled in the luxury of the copious steaming water. Then, he dried himself with one of the thick cotton towels that hung from a rack on the wall.

Beth was turning out the lights in the kitchen when she spotted a small book on a chair. As she picked it up, she realized it was Nikolai's pocket dictionary. Methodically, she tapped the small book against her palm and strode toward his room.

His door was slightly open. She knocked.

From inside, Beth heard him say, "Come."

She pushed the door open all the way. Nikolai stood in front of the bureau, putting folded clothes into a drawer. His back was to her, but she could see his reflection in the mirror, which hung above the bureau. His brushed hair still shone wet from the shower.

He was dressed in blue jeans and a soft flannel shirt that was unbuttoned, revealing his smooth sculptured chest and flat stomach. Just above the snap of the jeans, she could see a small forest of curly black hair that circled his belly button.

Beth drew in a quick breath, then averted her glance. When she looked up again, she found his soft, glistening eyes staring back at her from the mirror. She straightened and lifted her chin. "Here's your dictionary. I found it in the kitchen," she said, setting it on the bed.

"Thank you." His eyes remained fixed on her.

"No problem," Beth said. Then, she turned quickly and walked out of the room, closing the door behind her. She leaned her head back against the closed door as she exhaled a long breath.

What the hell was wrong with her? She had no business looking at him like that.

The last thing she needed right now was to give this guy the wrong idea and have him chasing after her, especially since her bedroom was just down the hall. She certainly had no interest in striking up a relationship with an uneducated peasant—no matter how old she got to be.

3

In her dark room, Beth began undressing. She stared out her window into the night, looking down at the low sun-sensor lights that glimmered in the frigid air. They lined the brick walks that bounded her mother's perennial gardens. The plants looked dead, but in the spring, they would again be the vibrant colorful flowers that the older woman had tended.

Beth was painfully aware her mother would not be alive to give them her loving care this coming spring. They would be orphaned plants just as she would be an orphaned daughter. She rested her forehead against the cold windowpane. *Who will care for me when my mother's gone?*

How lonely she felt amidst this planet full of people. Why could she not halt the freefalling solitary direction her life was taking?

Walking to the dresser, Beth removed her sweater, bra, and jeans, and put on a cotton nightgown that buttoned up the front. It hung open around her small but shapely body. As she stared into the mirror, she pulled the combs from her ash blonde hair and watched it tumble around her shoulders. She placed the palm of her hand across her breasts. They were full and warm, but they had never nourished a child, and it had been a long time since they had given pleasure to a man.

Smoothing her hand from her breasts down to her belly, her mind instantly conjured up the face of Nikolai with those translucent eyes and full, sensuous lips. The sight of his muscled chest and tapered waist flashed before her. She groaned in disgust and quickly buttoned the nightgown. Getting into bed, she pulled the covers up to her neck, vowing to rid herself of these ridiculous thoughts.

Nikolai awoke abruptly to the strong smell of coffee. He checked his alarm clock. It was already seven o'clock. He'd had no intention of sleeping this late, but the comfortable bed and the warmth of the room had lulled him into the kind of deep sleep he hadn't enjoyed since his days in Russia.

His dreams last night were another reason he had not wanted to awaken. He dreamed he was in his bed making passionate love. The woman's kisses scalded his lips, and her hands moved hotly on his chest and belly. In a desperate voice, she begged him to take her, which he did with passion equal to hers.

Unfortunately, as their ecstasy reached its explosive climax, he smelled the coffee and awoke. Not only was he alone in his bed, but the passionate woman of his dreams was none other than Beth Winters. He winced, remembering that in his waking hours, the woman's dislike of him was apparent.

He threw on a sweatshirt, jeans, and sneakers and rushed into the bathroom to brush his teeth and comb his hair. In the kitchen, Beth was leaning against the counter as she drank her coffee. Unlike her ardor in his dream, she barely spoke to him. Her disdain suited him perfectly because, to his chagrin, he found himself staring at her lips and breasts, which in turn caused him to feel aroused.

Beth turned away from him to put her cup into the sink and said, "You know what your jobs are for today. Please try to finish all of them."

Nikolai nodded.

"My mother is still sleeping. The home health aid will be here at eight o'clock to give her breakfast and bathe her.

Searching her purse for her keys, she added, "Oh, I'll talk to Amy Ressler, the English professor, to see when you can sit in on her English class."

He mumbled, "Thank you," but his words were lost in the sound of the door slamming shut behind her. He sat at the kitchen table with a cup of coffee. Running a hand through his dark hair, he tried to recall the passionate woman of his dreams.

As Nikolai pulled on his jacket and went out to begin his chores, he vowed to perform each job with such attention to detail that Beth would have to say something nice to him.

At lunchtime, he peeked in on Mrs. Winters who was being attended to by the health aid. The older woman seemed genuinely happy to see him. Buoyed by her kindness, he whistled through all of his afternoon work.

Beth pulled into the driveway at four o'clock and parked her car in the garage. As she walked toward the house, she surveyed the yard, which was immaculate. A noise in the cellar caught her attention. Entering the open hatchway, she found Nikolai putting away the last of the patio furniture.

"Everything okay?" he asked.

Her genuine relief and total satisfaction outweighed her dislike of him. She smiled broadly. "Everything looks wonderful. Thank you, Nikolai."

"I am glad I please you," he answered, also smiling.

Beth suddenly scowled at his words, which conjured up the scene of the night before when she pressed her hand against her body and unhappily found herself picturing his Greek god image at the same time. She turned and stalked off to cook.

Nikolai went to his room. In the shower, his anger surged. What did he have to do to please her? He had worked hard all day, but the minute he said something nice, she bristled. He braced himself solidly against the gushing water with his hands on his hips, trying to figure out which of his words had offended her. As he stood there naked, one thing was very obvious. Even angry thoughts of her caused him to become aroused.

He had not been with a woman since he had come from Russia; thus he assumed this peculiar "malady" was afflicting him because of his long period of abstinence. *Maybe I must go to a lady of the night. Perhaps that will get rid of this unwanted reaction,* he thought.

Nikolai dressed carefully for dinner that evening, choosing black jeans and his best gray cashmere sweater, which he had brought from Russia. He brushed his dark hair back. *At least I will make my appearance as favorable as possible since my personality seems to offend her.*

When Nikolai entered the kitchen, Beth was standing at the stove cutting up roasted chicken. Not looking at him, she said, "Tomorrow morning at nine o'clock I'll drive you to the university. Amy Ressler is going to let you join her class. After that, you can take the bus home and begin your work around the house."

As she turned and handed him his plate, he sat down at the kitchen table.

"Nikolai, don't you want to eat in my mother's room tonight?"

"Kitchen is better. I talk too much and make you angry," he answered as he stabbed at his food.

"Please join us. It will make Mother happy."

"And you?"

"Yes, I want you to come, but just don't talk about marriage."

Carrying food on a tray, Beth led the way into her mother's room. As she served her mother, she heard Nikolai settle into a chair.

The older woman said, "I hear you will spend the morning at the university tomorrow."

"Yes, Madam."

"I will miss you. It is such a comfort for me to know you are here if I need you."

"Then I not go, Madam," he said, as he again tilted his head slightly, reminding Beth of a dog they had once had who always cocked his head to the side while listening to his master's commands.

"Oh, no, you must go and learn English. You have a long life ahead of you and knowing English will be a great help to you." She spoke in a soft voice. "You know that I am not long for this world. The doctor says I only have a few more months to live, but I know I am going someplace special."

"You are right about special place. Someday all of us go there."

"So, you believe this, too?"

"Absolute, Madam."

"Beth does not believe in God or heaven."

Nikolai turned to Beth and in his probing, beautiful eyes she saw genuine compassion. "Why you not believe in place like heaven?"

"Because I can't see it," she retorted.

"Can you see . . . how do you say . . . gravity? Even can you hear special whistles dogs hear . . . no, you cannot. How small is human . . . wait, I find word in dictionary . . . ah, yes . . . *awareness.* Human awareness is tiny in whole universe. Today, even scientists believe there are . . . let me find word . . . hmm . . . yes . . . *dimensions* that humans cannot see. Maybe one dimension is resting place for souls. This is mathematical theory, not just crazy idea. You are small person in whole universe. You know nothing about its beautiful . . . let me find word . . . ah, yes . . . *mysteries.*"

Beth leaned back in her chair with her legs stretched out in front of her, one crossed over the other at the ankle. With her elbows resting on the arms of the chair and her fingertips coming together steeple-style up near her face, she wondered if it was such a good idea to teach him better English when he was already winning arguments in his limited style. It also crossed her mind that such matters should be beyond the ken of a handyman.

Studying him, she asked, "How do you know this stuff?"

Nikolai shrugged. "I read magazine on airplane to U.S."

"Well, I guess it's time we called it a night. You need to rest your brain for English class tomorrow." She stacked the dishes and headed for the door, waiting for Nikolai to open it.

Turning toward him, Beth saw her mother take Nikolai's hand and say, "Thank you for the wonderful explanation of the universe. It has helped me not to be afraid of the end."

"All life ends, Madam. Some sooner than others," he replied gently. Then he bent down and kissed her cheek.

Beth turned away, wondering when, in all the day-to-day caregiving, she had last given her mother even a peck on the cheek.

In the morning, Nikolai entered the kitchen and poured himself a cup of coffee. Beth was sitting at the table reading the newspaper. She put the paper down and removed her reading glasses as she looked up at him. "You'll have to drink that fast because I have to leave in about fifteen minutes."

He nodded and sat across from her. Since he had experienced another night of passion with Beth Winters in his dreams, he tried not to look at her, fearing an adverse reaction. Quickly, he finished his coffee and put on his jacket while she fished in her purse for her keys.

On the way to Fairfield University, Beth listened as Nikolai read road signs and billboards aloud, trying to pronounce the words correctly. As they drove by a restaurant, he sounded out the word "cocktails." His pronunciation of the first vowel of the word fell somewhere between *cocktail* and *cooktail.*

Beth pronounced the word as it should be said in English, but he insisted his pronunciation was right. "This is French word. Must say this way."

Beth continued, using the English pronunciation, "Cocktail means liquor mixed with something like soda or fruit juice."

"No, no," he insisted, "it is mixture of two liquids and one is milk. Liquor not necessary. This is French word—you must look in French dictionary."

Beth shook her head. *This is one stubborn bastard.*

Presently, a Pontiac passed them, and Nikolai pronounced the model name, "Grand Prix," sounding the *x* at the end of the word.

She pounced to correct him. "No, the word is pronounced Grand *Pree*." And delivering her strongest blow, Beth said, "It's a French word, so we don't pronounce the *x*." Then she clamped her mouth shut for the rest of the trip.

Nikolai gathered up his notebook and pen as Beth parked the car in the faculty parking lot. They walked a short distance to a large brick building. Inside the classroom, Nikolai noticed a few students gathered in the back of the room as he and Beth made their way to the front, where Amy was writing on the board.

Beth said, "Hi, Amy. This is Nikolai."

Putting down the chalk, she turned and extended a hand. "I'm so glad to meet you. Beth tells me you're from Russia."

Nikolai extended his hand.

"That's wonderful. It's such a beautiful country."

"You go to Russia?" he asked.

"Yes, to Moscow."

Beth interrupted, "I've got to go, Amy. I have a class."

"Oh, Beth, I want to thank you for taking my foreign student under your wing. I know you spent a lot of extra time with her."

"No problem."

"Well, all I know is a lot of these kids wouldn't graduate if you weren't doing what you do."

"Thanks. I try to help when I can. I'll see you later."

Amy turned to Nikolai and said, "Why don't you sit right there."

Nikolai nodded and moved toward the seat.

Beth said her goodbyes to Amy and left, giving Nikolai a lingering glance.

The other students took their seats, and Amy began to speak.

Nikolai studied her. She looked to be in her late twenties and was attractive. Although she was slightly heavy, she had a voluptuous figure which she accentuated with a rather tight sweater. Her pale skin contrasted her dark eyes and hair and the ruby-red lips.

Thinking about the involuntary arousals he had had when he was near Beth, Nikolai chewed on his lip, worrying that the same thing might happen if he remained in Amy Ressler's company too long. His fears were unfounded, however, because even though Ms. Ressler cooed over him in class and touched his shoulder, nothing happened.

In her mother's room that evening, Beth set her dinner plate on the small table next to her and looked over at Nikolai. "How was your class today? Did you like it?"

"Class was good, and teacher was very nice."

Beth studied him to see if she could discern exactly what he meant by "very nice," but his face was impassive. She asked, "What are you learning?"

"Some new words and some grammar. Grammar is confusing. Teacher say adjectives come before nouns, like example 'the blue dress.' Here adjective is blue and noun is dress."

"Yes, that's right. So what's the problem?"

"Well, what about sentence like, 'The dress is blue.' Now adjective come after noun."

"That's a different sentence construction."

Before Beth could explain, he continued, "Why all rules in English can be broken. This make English difficult. I not understand why English is international language. What world needs is new Lingua Franca that all people know."

Beth grabbed his Russian-English pocket dictionary which was lying on a small table near her and flipped it open. "Well, I hope to God that Russian words won't be included in this new language of yours. You think English is tough? Look at this." She thrust the open book with its Cyrillic alphabet under his nose. "These don't look like words, they look more like geometric equations."

Nonplused by her outburst, he went on, "World must have one language. You hear of Esperanto?"

"Yes, I have," she answered with rising irritation. "But it's not a real language. No country actually speaks it. It's just a language that some professors dreamed up. It's probably more like Pig Latin than anything else. And it certainly is not going to solve the communication problems of the world any time soon."

"What is Pig Latin?" he asked, again cocking his head.

Beth rolled her eyes in exasperation and snapped, "Never mind."

Mrs. Winters interceded, "Beth, Nikolai tells me that Amy Ressler can speak Russian and would like him to stay after class sometime so she can converse with him in the language."

Biting the inside of her lip, Beth turned back to Nikolai. "What did you tell her?"

"I tell her I must work at house. No time for talk."

When Beth heard his answer, for some strange reason, she felt relieved. She had to admit the idea of him spending time with Amy or any other woman bothered her even though he exasperated the hell out of her.

This was not the only strange reaction she'd had lately. Often, she found herself studying his face and admiring his lean, muscular body. Also, when she walked past his closed bedroom door, she would stop for a moment, listening to hear him moving around within. Although these reactions appeared to be trivial, she still considered them to be a breach of her strict code of conduct.

Lying in bed that night, Beth punched her pillow into a ball and wedged it behind her head. Was her brain turning to mush? Even as an adolescent, Beth had known what she wanted: first, to become a college English professor, and then to find a man to marry who was at least her equal intellectually and financially.

So why was she attracted to an immigrant peasant, who earned seven dollars an hour and also managed to piss her off royally every chance he got? Shutting her eyes, Beth pulled the pillow from behind her head and hugged it close to her chest. Instantly, the half-smiling face of Nikolai invaded her thoughts. She threw the pillow off the bed.

4

Nikolai decided to eat his lunch in Mrs. Winters' room every day. During this time, the health aid would leave them alone. One afternoon, the older woman asked, "Nikolai, do you believe in reincarnation?"

"Certainly, Madam."

She continued, "I know in India the people believe in it."

"Not only Indians believe this. Ancient Greeks believed in . . . let me look word up . . . ah yes . . . *transmigration.* Just like Indian belief, this word means after death, souls go to another body."

"Yes, but the ancient Greeks lived thousands of years ago."

"Even today, some scientists have theory maybe like reincarnation. You know burned-out stars?" he said as he leafed through his dictionary. "They called black holes. Scientists think some things floating in space be pulled into black hole. This stuff come out other end of black hole. And guess what happen next?"

"What?" Mrs. Winters asked, lifting her head off the pillow.

"Scientists think this stuff go to another universe or maybe come back here, but in another time or place."

"You mean like a time machine?" she asked with a gleam of amazement in her eyes.

"Yes, something like time machine. So, maybe after death our souls be pulled into black hole, then come out in different body in another time or place." He winked at her and added, "If this is so, I hope when we come back here next time, I am right age to be . . . let me find word . . . yes . . . *suitor.* I want to be suitor for you, beautiful lady."

Mrs. Winters burst out into the first laughter he had heard from her since he had come. She put out both of her arms, and he bent down to hug her. Looking at him with motherly love, she said, "Nikolai, you are an angel come to earth."

"Or maybe I am just some garbage cast out of black hole and sent here in this body."

The older woman laughed again. "Whatever or whoever you are, you do my heart good."

That evening, Beth came into her mother's room and handed Nikolai the screw driver he needed to put up a new window shade. She perched in a chair near her mother's bed, watching Nikolai as he balanced on a stepladder and worked on the shade. "Mom, do you know who I ran into today?"

"No, who?"

"Andrea Wilcox, remember her?"

"Oh, yes. How is she?"

"Not very happy. She's having trouble with her husband. He's an old fashioned boor who thinks he has to be the boss in the house just because he's the man even though he's not nearly as intelligent as Andrea."

"Beth, it's not the end of the world for a man to be in charge of his household," Mrs. Winters replied.

Beth watched while Nikolai applied some muscle to the screwdriver. He looked over his shoulder at them and said, "In past and today even, in some cultures man must be more powerful than woman in marriage."

"Even if he's stupid," Beth hissed as she put one hand on her hip.

Fuming, she skewered him with her eyes as he took a step down and sat on the top of the stepladder. He rested his arm on his thigh, tapping the screwdriver on his knee. "Every organization must have leader who everyone must listen to—army, business, church, and other. Person in charge is not always smartest, but others must listen because of his title. This is important for harmony. Marriage is not different. Most places in world, woman must . . . let me find word." He pulled his dictionary out of his pocket with his free hand and opened it to the Ds. "Ah . . . yes . . . *defer.* Woman must defer to husband."

"That's baloney. It's just an excuse you men use to get your own way."

"Just because women want power today, that not mean it is right—just different thinking from past. We not so different from ancient people. And wisdom from past is usually right."

"Not in this house," Beth shot back. "Where do you get this crap anyway?"

"Bible is ancient wisdom. It says woman must defer to husband's wishes."

Beth stood up, putting both hands on her hips, and glared at him. She was angry enough to spit. Not only had the provincial bastard pulled rank on her by bringing God into the argument, but what really aggravated her, was that his halting English made some sense.

Grabbing the screwdriver away from him, she stalked out of the room, thinking, *It's time to get this guy out of English class.*

As Beth poured herself a second cup of coffee the next morning, Nikolai came into the kitchen dressed for class. She was still peeved at him from the conversation the night before, but she found herself admiring his handsome face and broad shoulders. With apparently no remorse, he sipped his coffee and opened his notebook for a quick review of his homework.

He looked over at her. "When I use the verb "do," I think I must use "does" if subject of sentence is she?"

"Yes," she answered.

"Look at this. I write—I mean—I wrote these words from song on radio, but something is not right."

"Let me see it." She pulled the book toward her and read, "She don't get mad; she gets even."

"Well," Beth said, "this is definitely wrong. It should be, 'She doesn't get mad; she gets even.'"

Then taking the pencil, she wrote down the right verbs. "You know songs often don't have correct grammar. What station are you listening to, anyway?"

"The country station."

"Well, there's your trouble."

He brightened. "Your words, they are in a country song, too. Do you listen to this music, also?"

"I don't listen to that stuff, and you shouldn't either. It's going to confuse you. And besides, how can you even understand what they're talking about in those songs? They don't relate to life in Russia?"

"Life is life. Also, in Russia sometimes a man's dog dies, his wife leaves.

Only . . . he does not have pick-up truck."

Beth grabbed her car keys and led the way out the back door, shaking her head. *How does he always manage to get in the last word?*

Sunday morning, Beth sat at the kitchen table to jot down a grocery list, but she found herself doodling as thoughts of Nikolai invaded her mind. *Why isn't there one subject he and I can agree on? And how come he never concedes a point to me? I'm his boss for Christ's sake, but that doesn't intimidate him in the least.*

She knew it was she who was intimidated. He had this European way of standing too close when he talked to her, and he wasn't afraid to put his hands on her if it helped to prove his point. He wasn't self conscious about where he placed his hands, either.

She remembered one conversation when Nikolai was talking about the theory of evolution. He came very close to her and placed one hand on her back at the waist as he jabbered something about the human vertebrae. Then he placed the palm of his other hand on the left side of her belly where the appendix might be, adding that this organ was not necessary for modern man.

With him standing over her, both hands on her body, she had felt very warm and breathless, almost dizzy. Her mind shouted, *Step back away from him,* but she couldn't seem to move. She tried to steady herself, placing her palms against his chest. His head came down to hers, and his hands moved to her waist. Those translucent eyes drew her in, and his full sensuous lips hovered close above hers. It took all of her strength to step back and break the spell.

Now, instead of making a grocery list, she drew a line down the middle of the paper and labeled one side "good points," and the other "bad points." The good list read: "handsome, capable, sexy, compassionate." The list of bad points read: "pig-headed (which she underlined twice), overbearing, egotistical, poor, peasant, and not intellectual.

The last quality, however, she was not sure about. Just when she thought he was the most small-minded person she had ever met, he'd come out with some far-flung theory or ancient wisdom.

As he strolled into the kitchen buttoning the cuffs of his shirt and emitting heavenly scented cologne, Beth quickly folded the sheet of paper and stuffed it into the pocket of her jeans.

His eyes followed her motion, and he looked at her questioningly.

"My grocery list," she lied, pushing the paper deeper into her pocket.

"Can I put some things on list?" he asked.

"No. Just tell me what you want," she blurted out having the feeling he knew darn well it wasn't a grocery list.

Freezing rain pelted the ground as Beth drove Nikolai to his Monday morning English class. "When you get back to the house, don't forget to put my mother's quilt into the washing machine. I'll be home right after I go to the market," she said as she concentrated on the heavy morning traffic ahead of her.

Pushing strands of hair off her forehead, she added, "I just hope I can remember what we need."

"What about grocery list? You know the one from pocket of your jeans?" he asked, with a raised eyebrow.

Beth bit her lip. Last night she had put her blue jeans on the washing machine and had checked the pockets. Pulling out the list, she left it still folded on top of the jeans. Beth knew Nikolai would have to move them and the note to open the washer. She thought to herself, *He wouldn't dare read it.* But as she glanced at him sitting in the passenger seat, with a sly smile, she decided he just might.

When Nikolai's English class ended, he picked up his notebook and pen and walked toward the door, but Amy Ressler called out, stopping him. "Please wait for me, Nikolai."

He stood to one side as the other students filed out of the class, hoping he would not miss his bus. Finally, she was at his side, and they walked out of the room together.

"Nikolai, I would really like to converse with you in Russian. I need the practice. Don't you have any time in your schedule to do that?"

"Miss Ressler, I want to help, but I must work at the Winters'."

"Please call me Amy, and I'm sure Beth would give you time off for this."

"I will ask, but I must go now. Bus will be here soon."

"Listen, have a cup of coffee with me in the cafeteria. We can speak a little Russian, and then I will drive you to Beth's. You'll be home before the bus could get you there."

Not knowing what else to do, Nikolai followed her into the cafeteria. They were halfway through the coffee when Beth Winters came in with some friends.

Nikolai's blood froze in his veins. He had the feeling that if she saw him sitting here with the teacher, she would not be happy. He was supposed to be home at work.

Then the worst happened; Beth noticed him. Her angry stare showed plainly she was not happy to see him here, but when she saw he was having coffee with Amy, a different, but equally negative emotion transformed her face. She came over to them and glowered at Nikolai.

She hissed, "I thought you were supposed to catch the bus home, so you could finish your work. I'm not paying you to sit and drink coffee."

"Please, don't blame him, Beth," interjected Amy. "It's my fault. He told me he had to get home, but I wanted to practice using my Russian with someone who spoke the language on a formal level, and of course, Nikolai does. And just as soon as we've finished our coffee, I'll take him home."

Beth said crisply, "That won't be necessary. I'm going home in a few minutes to check on my mother."

"Please sit down with us," Amy said. "We're having the most enlightening conversation."

Beth sat stiffly, checking her watch as Amy and Nikolai conversed in Russian. After a few minutes, she stood up. "Well, we better be going. I don't want to be late for my next class."

Nodding to Amy, Nikolai got up.

She smiled. "I've enjoyed our conversation tremendously, and I hope we can do this again."

"I, too, enjoy this time, but I must work. You know . . ." The rest of the sentence he spoke in Russian.

Amy laughed and nodded as she translated his words. "That's right, Nikolai, 'Money is coined liberty.'"

Beth glared at Nikolai. "Have you read Dostoevsky?"

He studied the floor. "No, these are some words I hear."

Neither of them spoke as she drove him home. Nikolai worked his jaw muscles into an angry knot. When they reached the house, he got out of the car and nodded to her grimly as he shut the door behind him. She backed out of the driveway, without checking her mother, he noticed, and headed back toward the school.

Beth's harsh words circled in the back of her mind all through her afternoon classes. On the way home, stuck in rush hour traffic, she pondered the events in the cafeteria. Why had she acted so angrily? There was nothing wrong with Nikolai and Amy having coffee and speaking Russian in the cafeteria, and she knew Nikolai would finish whatever work he was supposed to do by working later if he had to. Then, she wondered how a peasant carpenter could speak formal Russian and quote Dostoevsky off the top of his head?

When Beth arrived at the house, Nikolai was just finishing up in the basement. Again, she was overwhelmed by the fastidiousness of his work and told him so in a conciliatory tone, but he would not look at her and simply said, "I not take lunch break to make up for time in cafeteria."

She started to say that wasn't necessary, but the words drifted in the air, unheard, as he stalked up the stairs to his room.

Shaking her head, she went into the kitchen to start dinner. When she was certain he had finished taking his shower, she walked down the hall and knocked at his door. Again his response was, "Come," but this time it was a little gruffer.

She took a deep breath and entered the room. He was standing by the bed adjusting the time on his alarm clock. He was again wearing the flannel shirt, which was mercifully buttoned.

"Nikolai, I know you're angry with me about today. Whatever I did wrong, I want to apologize," she said, speaking quickly.

He looked over at her with a scowl and tossed the small clock onto the bed. "You do not know why I am angry?" he asked almost menacingly as he walked toward her with his hands on his hips. "In front of that woman you talk to me like I am not human."

He stood dangerously close and glared down at her. "I work for you, yes, but I am not slave."

Beth was overcome by a multitude of emotions, most of which she could not identify. She tried to speak, but at that moment, she knew she was going to cry. So she put her hands up to her face and turned to leave the room.

Nikolai reached out, stopping her with one strong arm. As she burst into tears, he pulled her close and rubbed her back in a soothing motion. Enfolded in the warmth of his arms, she was surprised to find she felt safe and somehow loved.

She leaned her head against his chest, sobbing. When the crying subsided, he sat down on the bed with her and gave her his handkerchief to dry her eyes. Then he draped one arm around her shoulders. "Everything okay. Do not cry."

Dabbing her eyes, she looked up at him and began to speak, "Nikolai, I am truly sorry for the way I treated you today. It wasn't right. You did nothing wrong. My only defense for my actions is that I've been under a lot of stress. I worry about my mother. I must go to work and take care of the house and bills—everything's my responsibility. I'm just overwhelmed."

Again the tears began. Nikolai pulled her close. "You are only one small woman. You cannot do all things, must only do what you can. I am here. I will help. Not to worry, beautiful woman."

Getting control of herself, she stood, still clutching the handkerchief. He stood too, and took both of her hands in his. He placed them against his heart. "It is fate—that I be here with you now. I take your burdens." Then he raised her hands to his lips and kissed them.

Beth managed a smile. "Thank you, Nikolai."

A few evenings later, Beth trotted down the basement stairs with a basket of laundry on her hip. As she opened the washing machine, she noticed a folded piece of paper lying on top. She picked it up and unfolded it. The words, written in Nikolai's fancy European style, formed two lists. The first one was titled "Good Points." It read: "pretty, beautiful body, smart." The list titled "Bad Points" was a little longer, and it read: "stubborn, too much interested in money and position, cannot recognize intellectual man when he stands in front of her."

When she read the list of the good points, a heated flush surged through her as she thought of Nikolai studying her face and body in such an intimate way and a sense of pride surfaced as she read the word "smart". When Beth read the bad points, however, she wondered if she did possibly place too much emphasis on money and position.

In addition, she was sure she had grossly misjudged Nikolai in the area of intelligence. Just last week, she had peeked into his room while he was outside and was perplexed to see a book that translated scientific terms from Russian to English.

She leaned an elbow on the washing machine and rested her chin in her upturned palm as she methodically tapped the side of the note against the white enamel. She would have to reconsider her perceptions of Nikolai.

It was also time she assessed her feelings for him. He was on her mind more and more. It was as if he had become an obsession. Did she want a romantic involvement with a carpenter/handyman? Was he the kind of man who could share a full, rich, intellectual life with her?

Well, she thought, *maybe I should start dating some eligible bachelors. I'm not getting any younger, and I really have to decide what I want in a husband.*

Beth knew one of the professors at the university was interested in her. Maybe she would stop in to see him.

5

On Saturday at supper, as Beth set her mother's tray in front of her, she looked over at Nikolai. "I'm going out this evening. Can you sit with mother while I'm gone?"

"Of course."

"Where are you going?" asked her mother.

"To the ballet. We're going to see *Swan Lake*."

Both Nikolai and Mrs. Winters turned to look at Beth.

"Brad Wilson, from the science department, asked me to go. He'll be here about seven."

When the dishes were put in the dishwasher and the kitchen was tidy, Beth went to her room to get ready. She showered and dressed with care. She chose a fitted black dress with a v-neck that showed some cleavage. Four-inch black heels and pearl earrings put the final touches on the outfit. Carefully, Beth applied rose-colored lipstick.

Beth entered her mother's room and laid her coat on the back of a chair. The older woman gasped. "Oh, how beautiful you look, Beth. Doesn't she, Nikolai?"

Beth noticed his voice seemed to catch in his throat, but his face was an implacable mask that showed no sign of emotion.

The doorbell rang, and Beth jumped up to answer it. As she opened the front door, Brad Wilson, holding a bouquet of roses, smiled broadly. Tall and blonde, he was stunningly handsome in a dark suit, starched white shirt, and subdued tie. His teeth were so perfect he looked like he should be in an advertisement for toothpaste. She took the flowers he offered and led him into her mother's room.

Beth said, "Mother, I'd like you to meet Brad Wilson. He teaches advanced physics at the university."

Her handsome date took Mrs. Winters' hand in a grandiose gesture as he bent deeply over her hospital bed.

Beth continued with the introductions. "Brad, this is Nikolai Mendeleyev. He is helping me care for my mother."

Brad looked thoughtful and held out his hand to shake Nikolai's. "Hmm . . . Mendeleyev . . . Mendeleyev. I don't suppose you would know of the noted Russian physicist by that name. No, of course, you wouldn't."

Nikolai ignored the hand he extended. "No, I have not heard of this Mendeleyev." Then he added, "What area of physics is your—how do you say—specialty?"

"Astro-physics, actually," Brad answered, smiling.

Nikolai leaned back in his chair. "You have, then, experience with high energy particle accelerator?"

"Not exactly," answered Brad, stammering.

"So," Nikolai continued, "You do not work with matter-antimatter pair?"

"Not exactly." Brad was now looking thoroughly uncomfortable.

This is getting ridiculous, Beth thought. Picking up her coat, she said quickly, "We have to go. We don't want to be late for the ballet. See you later."

After Beth and Brad left, Nikolai stood up and looked out the window. Scowling, he watched the happy couple walk to the car.

However, when he turned around, his countenance softened. He smiled at Mrs. Winters and asked, "Do you know story of *Swan Lake*?"

"No."

He pulled his chair close to her bed. And with a twinkle in his eyes and intrigue in his voice, he said, "Then I must tell you."

He grabbed his dictionary to look up unfamiliar words and began, "The story is about young prince named Siegfried. His father dead, so when he is old enough, he must rule kingdom. Siegfried likes hunting and having parties—he does not want to be serious. On the day before Siegfried must become king, mother tells him he must find woman to marry. He must find this girl in one day. He is not happy because he loves no one.

"That night his friends say, 'Let us go hunting.' They go down to lake in the moonlight and see beautiful swans. One swan coming toward Siegfried has . . . let me find word . . . ah, yes . . . *crown*. Swan has crown on head. At midnight, the swan turns into beautiful girl. When Seigfried ask how she can go from swan to human, the girl, named Odette, says that evil magician changed her and her friends to swans, but he let them be human from midnight to when sun come up. The spell can be broken only if a man promise to love her forever.

"Siegfried knows he loves her and tells her he will marry her and stay with her all days of his life. They say they meet next night at midnight, but later Siegfried remembers he must be at ball at that time, choosing wife. Next night at the ball, Siegfried's mother angry because he will not take any lady there for wife.

"Suddenly, strange man appears. His name Count von Rothbart. He brings his daughter, named Odile. This woman looks just like swan maiden, Odette. The prince rushes to her and calls her his queen. He so . . ." Again, Nikolai opened his dictionary and leafed through it. "He so *entranced* with girl that he not hear desperate swan outside flapping wings at the window.

"The count says if Siegfried loves his daughter, then he must swear never to love other woman. Siegfried promises to love only Odile. Suddenly, lightning hits castle and Odile's face becomes like skeleton and father becomes owl. Siegfried sees swan flapping its wings outside castle and knows he has been tricked. He runs to her, but she is gone.

"He very unhappy. He goes to lake. Later, Odette comes to him. They embrace, but owl comes after them. Siegfried asks, 'How can we be safe?'

"She says, 'We cannot be safe. Since you promise love to Odile, I cannot be yours. So, I rather die.' Odette throws herself into lake and drowns. Then Siegfried jumps into lake. Both together forever. Their love stronger than magic of evil owl/magician.

Nikolai smiled. "Theme of story is true love stronger than evil, and also that things not always the way they seem."

Mrs. Winters turned her head on the pillow to look at him. "Something makes me think you are not exactly the person we think you are, Nikolai. Am I right?"

He looked at her with a grin, then stared down at his hands for a moment. "You are right."

"Please tell me about your life."

"This I can do, but you must not tell Beth what I say to you."

"On my honor," Mrs. Winters promised, placing her hand on her heart.

Slowly, he began, "I am not carpenter. I had high position in university in my country, but I had to leave."

"Why?"

"Government wanted me to work on deadly weapons project like my father. If I refuse they will send me to prison camp in Siberia, but I cannot do this."

"Why did you refuse?"

Nikolai rested his elbows on the arm of the chair. As he laced his fingers together, he stared at them. "I believe science should be for good only, not for bad."

"You're right. But how did you get away?" Mrs. Winters asked.

"I trick Russian KGB agents and sneak on big boat. When boat docked in New Haven, I disappear, but I have no papers or passport. Still, I must find job because my mother in Russia needs money. Russian friends here help me to find job at diner. Owner paid me very little money, but I must accept it. When diner closed, I come here to work."

"Why didn't you try to get asylum in this country?"

"It is not possible. Your government and government in my country made very secret deal. They . . ." he opened his dictionary and finding the word, he said, "*collaborate* to get all nuclear . . ." flipping some pages, he finished, "Oh yes, nuclear *material* out of countries that were part of Soviet Union. This take years. During this time, U.S. agree to send all Russian defectors back to Russia."

Mrs. Winters frowned. "Are you sure about this, Nikolai?"

He nodded solemnly. "Russian sailors try to defect one year ago, but when they escape, U.S. officials bring them back to Russian ship."

The older woman leaned back against her pillow and sighed. "Oh my goodness. So you aren't safe here or there."

"This is true."

"But why don't you tell Beth all of this?"

"I do not want Beth to know I am not legal. It will give her trouble as my employer."

"But, you could tell her about your background as a professor."

Nikolai hesitated. "Then she would ask why I do this low work if I am big professor. Also, I want that Beth accept me as I am—as carpenter."

Shifting in her bed, Mrs. Winters tilted her head to one side. "Do you care for her?"

"Yes." He sat back in his chair, looking down at his steepled fingers.

"If you don't tell her the truth, you may lose her."

"At this moment, it is what I must do."

Mrs. Winters looked at him. "Beth needs you, Nikolai. I know she spouts all this stuff about being an independent woman, but she needs a strong man like you."

"Maybe she will marry Brad."

"I don't think so. You pretty much shattered the image she had of him with the questions you put to him."

"For this, I am glad."

Mrs. Winters smiled and reached for his hand.

He kept his hand in hers until she dozed, then went to his room and lay on the bed. His mind raced. Nikolai imagined Brad kissing Beth and holding her in his arms. As these scenarios played over and over in his mind, he jumped off the bed and paced.

He stood looking out the window. When the lights of a car flashed along the grass and stopped, Nikolai recognized his cousin's black sedan. He put on his jacket and stole out of the house, not wanting to wake Mrs. Winters.

Peering into the open window of the car, he spoke in a low voice. "Sergei, it is very late."

The man took a pack of unfiltered Camels from his shirt pocket and tapped one out and offered one to Nikolai. He spoke in rapid Russian. "I know. That is why I did not call the house, but I had to talk to you."

"What is it?"

"I have learned news about the false papers."

Nikolai got into the passenger seat and closed the door. "When can we get them?" he asked.

"The end of the month on Friday night. Make sure you can get the time off. We may have only one chance."

"Why must we wait so long?" Nikolai asked, taking a drag on the cigarette.

"The building was just raided by the police, so our comrades must find a new place to set up. That will take time."

"Were arrests made?"

"Very many. The police surrounded the building, so no one could get away. Those caught are being held until they are deported."

Nikolai looked out the window and bit his lip. "We have no choice. We must do this." Then, he stubbed the cigarette out in the ashtray.

Back inside, Nikolai took up his post by the window. As he watched for Beth's return, his mind wandered. Trying to get these papers was a dangerous enough business, but if he were caught, deportation would mean a Siberian prison camp, and Beth would be an untouchable dream.

At midnight, Brad's car pulled into the driveway. He walked Beth to the front door. Nikolai could not see them from his vantage point, and he was happy that Brad left quickly.

Nikolai listened as Beth unlocked the door and made her way down the hall. He heard her stop for a moment outside his door, then go to her own room. He tossed restlessly in his bed and finally got up and padded barefoot to the kitchen, dressed in a pair of sweat pants and the unbuttoned flannel shirt.

He was sitting in a kitchen chair with his elbows on the table and a steaming mug before him when Beth came in. She was wearing a soft flannel nightgown with lace at the neck and sleeves.

Even without the fancy clothes and makeup, she looked beautiful. She sat down opposite him and leaned an elbow on the table, resting her chin in her palm. "What are you drinking?"

"Hot chocolate. You would like some?"

"Yes, please," she answered.

He swung out of his chair and fixed her a mug of the hot liquid. "How was ballet?"

"It was nice."

"And date, how was that?" he asked, sitting back down.

"It was okay."

"Only okay?"

"Yes, thanks to you. When Brad couldn't answer your questions, I think he must have felt embarrassed because after that he spent most of the evening trying to impress me with his academic credentials." Then looking at Nikolai, Beth asked, "How do you know that scientific stuff, anyway?"

"I have book of these words translated into English."

"But why would you want to know them?" she asked, frowning.

He shrugged. "I am interested."

She chewed on her lip as she drummed her fingertips on the side of the mug.

"Give me your hands," he said, reaching out for them.

She hesitated a moment, then extended them toward him.

He took them in his own and lightly rubbed his thumbs over the tops of her fingers and down over her nails. Then he turned her hands over and smoothed his thumbs over her palms.

He said, "Do you know that the hands can tell much about a person?"

Beth laughed, looking flushed. "Well, what are my hands telling you?"

"Many things . . . even little things. Look, there is space between little finger and next one. This means you fear small places or someone have control over you."

Beth gave him a patronizing glance.

Setting down her left hand, he concentrated on the right. He gently tried to move her thumb sideways. When the joint resisted movement, he smiled. "This means stubborn."

Beth made an amused face.

He deftly moved his thumb across her upper palm and said, "Your heart line. This line tells about feelings of love. See how it goes up toward first finger? That means you want husband with money and position. You think he must be perfect and you also. But when you marry, you will be faithful to husband forever."

"You're trying to tell me you can read all of that from this one line?"

Nikolai ignored the comment and continued to stare into her palm. He ran his thumb over the middle line. "This is the head line. You have strong one. This means you think clearly and understand difficult things."

He fingered the line that made a large semi-circle around her thumb. "And this is life line. It begins here, close to thumb and shows . . . how do you say . . . persistence. See these small lines that cross it? They mean stress and problems but also wisdom that comes with them."

Then taking in the entire palm, he said, "Hand is pink and healthy-looking. That shows that person can love another very much and also wants to be loved."

He continued to gently stroke her palm. "Your hand tells your life." He looked up at her and met her gaze.

She stared into his eyes, while he held her hand that quavered like a captured fish as she withdrew it from both of his.

She rested her elbows on the table and settled her chin onto her clasped hands. "Nikolai, how do you know about this?"

"My grandmother from Bukhara—her ancestors have some gypsy blood." As he spoke, he noticed her eyes strayed from his face down to his chest, where the open flannel shirt left it exposed, and her gaze lingered there.

When Beth glanced up at him, their eyes met. She pushed away the half-full mug and stood. "Well, I guess I'll go to bed."

"Sleep well, my love," Nikolai whispered as she marched down the hall to her room.

6

The next afternoon, Nikolai read the newspaper to Mrs. Winters. He finished with the "Dear Abby" column. The woman writing in was complaining about her son.

Mrs. Winters sighed. "I just don't understand how children can be so opposite of their parents. Look at Beth. Her whole philosophy of life is different from mine."

Smiling, Nikolai settled his eyes on hers. "Although children come from parents and learn from parents, they do not always understand each other. But, still there is love, and family will be together in bad times."

It had been snowing lightly, and large snowflakes settled on the windowsill. Nikolai bounced out of his chair and picked up the older woman's empty teacup. He walked over to the window, and opening it a little, he set the teacup on the sill. After a moment, the pristine white flakes accumulated.

Then Nikolai retrieved it and closed the window. Taking the magnifying glass that Mrs. Winters used to decipher small print, he held it over the cup, showing her the precise crystalline pattern of each snowflake.

The older woman gasped, surveying the myriad unique sparkling shapes.

He smiled. "All snowflakes different, but all are snow. It is the same with families."

"That's true, and I know Beth loves me and loved her father, but she never accepted the roles we had in our marriage."

Nikolai smoothed his mustache with the deliberate motion of his thumb and index finger. "Beth is proud to be modern woman, and for her respect is important. When she finds man she can respect, she will understand what you did."

Mrs. Winters touched his arm. "I think you're right, Nikolai."

In the days that followed, Beth's mother suffered greater pain, and stronger pills had to be given every two hours. Although Nikolai spent more time with the older woman during the day, it was Beth who stayed in the sick room at night and awoke to administer medication.

One evening as they stood over Mrs. Winters' bed, Beth suddenly felt faint and grasped Nikolai's arm.

"What is wrong?" he asked.

"I'm feeling a little dizzy. I better lie down."

Nikolai put his arm around her and helped her to her room. After he laid her down, he took off her shoes. Sitting on the bed, he said, "Beth, you must get sleep. Tomorrow you must teach. I will sleep in mother's room in recliner. When she wakes up, I will take care of her."

"Thank you, Nikolai," she said, looking up at him.

"Rest now," he replied, placing his hand in the hollow of her neck and massaging her cheek with his thumb.

Basking in his golden gaze, she would have given anything to pull his head down to hers for the briefest taste of those beautiful lips.

Feeling overwhelmed, Beth hired a cleaning woman to come to the house every other week. Nikolai, however, cleaned his own room. He kept it spotless and spare. Only a few items adorned his bureau.

These included an alarm clock and a small radio that played disks. On his night table were two photos in antique silver frames. One was of an older couple, who Beth assumed were his parents, and another was of a young woman. This second picture was set upon a fancy lace handkerchief, which lay flat, serving as a doily.

One day while Nikolai worked in the cellar, Beth stole into his room and picked up the picture of the young woman. She studied the beautiful face with its delicate features, and then fingered the hand-crocheted edge of the handkerchief. *Who was this woman and what was she to Nikolai?* Besides the fact that he was a carpenter and that he had a sick mother, she really knew nothing about him.

And lately there were mysterious meetings late at night in his cousin's black car. Beth could make out their profiles as their lighted cigarettes illuminated the interior.

Then there were the phone conversations. Her telephone bill listed one or two calls to Russia a month, which Nikolai promptly gave her the money for. From his room, Beth could hear him speaking quietly into the phone. She wondered if he was talking to his mother or a woman . . . maybe the woman in the picture.

Often after these phone calls, Beth could hear strains of Russian classical music, and it occurred to her he might be homesick. She often wondered how a peasant carpenter could know involved scientific terms, understand philosophy, and appreciate classical music.

While she was making coffee in the kitchen the next evening, Nikolai sat at the table doing his homework. He said, "I have some vocabulary words I do not know. What does word 'dilemma' mean?"

"It means having a problem," Beth answered.

"How do I use it?"

"Well, how about this sentence. Russians have a dilemma when they drink too much vodka."

He laughed. "It is not dilemma for Russians . . . only those around them." Then he added, "How about the word 'engross'? How do I use that?"

"Engross means to be totally involved with something or someone," she answered.

Tapping the side of the pencil to his lips, he said, "Then I can say I am engrossed with a woman?"

"Yes, you could," she answered. And a moment later, she asked, "Are you?"

"Am I what?"

She ignored his question. "Who is the woman in the picture on your bureau?"

"Why do you ask?"

"Why do you always have to answer a question with a question?" she demanded hotly. "Can't you ever just give me a straightforward answer?"

"She was my sister," he said as he lowered his chin on his folded hands.

"What do you mean—*was*? Did she pass away?"

"Yes." He looked up at her with a steadfast stare.

"Oh, I'm so sorry. I shouldn't have brought it up," she said, standing up and bringing her hands up to her cheeks in agitation.

He got up. "It is all right. She died many years ago."

He came close to her. Taking her wrists, he pressed her hands to his chest. "To answer your first question . . . Yes, I am engrossed with a woman. I desire her very much, and I think she wants me."

Those translucent eyes held her fixed as his mouth hovered dangerously close to hers. She did not flinch or turn her head away as their parted lips met. Hungrily, he devoured her mouth and pulled her tightly against him.

Beth threw her arms around him with the same reckless need. She moaned as his kisses scalded her neck, and he buried his face in her hair. This was the climax to all of her thoughts about him since he had come to her home, and every fiber of her being wanted to take this moment to its predictable ending, but she couldn't. He worked for her. She didn't want to marry a carpenter/handyman. If they consummated the relationship, how could they ever get back to the employer/employee relationship?

She pushed against his chest. "Nikolai, no . . . I can't do this."

He wrenched away from her. "You *can* do this. Problem is you *will not* do this because you think I am not good enough for you!" Then, in a tirade of Russian, he turned and stalked off to his bedroom.

Beth's mind reeled. She knew he was right. If he had a degree or traveled in the right social circles, she would welcome his advances. Then, she thought of his dead sister. She ran to his room and pushed open the door without knocking. He was taking off his T-shirt and stood there naked from the waist up.

Feeling her eyes mist, she said, "Nikolai, I am so sorry about your sister, and I'm sorry about everything else. This whole thing was my fault. It shouldn't have happened."

His glance softened. "It is not your fault that I desire you. That is my problem, and I will control it. Do not worry. I will not touch you again. As for my sister, she is gone. We can do nothing about that."

Wiping tears from her eyes, Beth asked, "You won't leave, will you, Nikolai? I need you."

He went to her and placed a hand on her shoulder. "I will not leave you."

Looking down at her, he added, "Do you know that some physicists believe in Many Worlds Theory?" This theory means that our world is always splitting into . . . let me remember . . . yes . . . identical worlds, where there is twin of us. We cannot see these worlds that exist next to our own, but when we decide to do one action here, our twin in other dimension is doing opposite action. So even though you will not let me make love to you here, I am certain that I make love to you there."

Beth flushed at the thought of them having sex even if it were in another world, but all she said to him was, "Nikolai, I don't know where you get these preposterous theories."

"You must believe me; it is scientific theory."

Beth shook her head, but increasingly she was harboring genuine feelings of respect and admiration for him. She was impressed at how quickly he was becoming proficient in English and how knowledgeable he was in almost every subject they talked about.

She was also impressed with his uncanny ability to forge an amalgam of science, philosophy, and literature and turn it into a credible argument for which she had no response. Besides this growing respect, there was the fiery passion for him that leapt up in her at a moment's notice.

7

On a Friday evening in the middle of December, Nikolai dressed in dark clothes. Pulling open a drawer, he took out a roll of money and leafed through it—all he'd saved since being robbed. He put it in a pocket inside his jacket and looked around this "woman's room" where he had been so comfortable since he began working here. If he did not return, there would be no comfort for him, physically or emotionally. He picked up the picture of his sister and ran a thumb lovingly over the glass. Pulling on his jacket, he turned out the light and closed the door softly behind him.

He peeked into Mrs. Winters' room, and his eyes stung with tears as he watched her sleep peacefully. Then zipping his jacket, he walked into the library where Beth was correcting papers. When she looked up at him, the soft beauty of her face tore at his heart.

He wanted to touch her hair and hold her close, but he only said, "I must go out for a while with my cousin. I don't know how long our business will take."

"What kind of business can you do at this time of night?" Her brow furrowed.

"Russians are always ready to do business," he said, trying to joke.

"Well, you have your key," she said, almost as a question.

Giving her a long look, he nodded and then turned toward the front door.

In the driveway, Nikolai slid into Sergei's car. The heavy-set man pulled a handgun from his pocket and spoke in rapid Russian. "I brought this in case we need it."

"Is the gun for the police if they raid the building or for the thugs making our identification?"

"A little of both." He smiled. "I do not trust anyone, not even our contact."

"Where are we going?"

"To an abandoned warehouse in the city."

"How long will it take?"

"Maybe an hour and a half."

"We must have our wits about us in case there is a raid."

"Of course, but just think what a different life we will have. We will be able to get higher-paying jobs. Of course your life won't be like it was in Russia, but it will be much better than it is now."

Nikolai lit a cigarette and thought, *How tolerable would life be if he could not see Beth everyday.*

They drove to an abandoned factory on the Lower East Side. The windows of the dilapidated building were painted black, but a glimmer of light shone through scratched areas.

As they slowly cruised past, Sergei said, "This is the place."

"It does not look very inviting," Nikolai answered.

Sergei circled the block again. "We do not have a choice. You don't want to be a handyman for the rest of your life, do you?"

He parked in a side alley a short distance away.

"I just hope we can get in and out without trouble," Nikolai said as he opened the car door.

Sergei stubbed out his cigarette. "We will be okay. We will get our documents and leave quickly."

Nikolai nodded.

They entered the building through a heavy metal door and went up a concrete stairway. They trudged to the top floor which opened into a huge room.

As they entered the large open area, crowded with throngs of people, the two men surveyed the space . . . the high ceilings, tall blackened windows, and bare light bulbs hanging from long cords. Next to make-shift wooden counters and stacks of files in open plastic crates, fax machines, copy machines, and laminating machines hummed with the brisk business.

Digital cameras constantly flashed as nervous-looking men and women waited their turn to receive their phony documents. Business appeared to be good as money materialized and fake social security cards, driver's licenses, and green cards were passed in exchange.

A burly-looking man, dressed in a black leather jacket and black jeans pushed them forward and said in crude Russian, "Pay over there first."

As they moved toward the dilapidated desk with the young dark-haired woman sitting behind it, Sergei said to Nikolai, "They tell me a person can even get a fake divorce here. Then for $25,000 dollars, they will even find an American to marry you so you won't be deported."

Nikolai continued to survey the room. He poked Sergei and said under his breath, "The exit to the roof is over there."

They were almost at the desk when the heavy metal door flew open, and police burst in, aiming semi-automatic rifles and yelling, "Freeze." In the panic and screaming, Nikolai and Sergei bolted through the exit door to the roof. Someone yelled, "Get them!"

They scrambled up the stairs and emerged out on the roof, out of breath and trembling. From within, they could hear the running footsteps of their pursuers.

Back to back, they frantically scanned the rooftop for a way off. Nikolai pointed to the top of a metal fire escape ladder.

They rushed to the ladder, Sergei swinging onto it first with Nikolai close behind. They could hear the police on the roof and see the frantic flashlight beams above them.

Nikolai yelled to Sergei, "Slide the rest of the way!" The two men placed the soles of their shoes on the outer edges of the metal ladder and slid to the ground. Once they reached the bottom, they sprinted into the dark alley.

Running full speed, they reached the car and sped away. Sergei pounded the steering wheel. "I can't believe it. We were so close."

Nikolai ran a hand through his hair. "At least they didn't get our money or us."

Beth heard the car pull up in front of the house. She slid out of bed and peeked out the window but could only see the glow of lighted cigarettes within. It was well after midnight. Where had he gone? Were they out with women? She crawled back into bed chiding herself for caring.

The next day, as he worked through his chores, his thoughts revolved around the close call of the night before. Was this social security card worth the danger? He knew it would guarantee him a better job and even give him a chance to go to college here, but he shivered at the thought of a Siberian prison.

Amy Ressler had told him about CLEG tests which allowed a person to take a preliminary test for a certain course, and if he passed, he could skip the course and move up to the next level.

The possibility of becoming a professor again thrilled him, but did he want to leave this house and Beth? He ran a hand over his face and thought, *The future will bring the solution.*

Beth held the six-foot Christmas tree vertical as Nikolai secured the trunk in the stand. She stood back and surveyed it. "It looks straight to me."

He studied it. "It is a good tree." Then he turned to her. "Do you want me to help to decorate it before your friends come?"

Beth sorted through the brightly colored bulbs. "No. I have plenty of time to put up the garland and the ornaments. You can finish your homework."

He nodded and headed for his room.

After Beth had put up most of the decorations, she stood back and looked at the tree. It needed something.

Going into the hallway, she called Nikolai. He opened his door and stuck his head out. "You need me?"

"Yes. I want to put a few more finishing touches on the tree. Can you get that last box?"

"Okay," he said, coming out of his room. He reached for the looped rope of the ceiling attic door and pulled it open. After searching for a few minutes, he carried down the plastic bin, setting it near the tree. "Is this the one?"

"Yes. Thanks."

As Beth looked through it, she saw an old shoe box tucked at the bottom. Opening it, she found intricate snowflake ornaments her mother had crocheted. They hadn't adorned their Christmas trees for many years.

Beth's eyes filled with tears, remembering the Christmas she and her mother were decorating the tree. When her mother pulled out the delicate snowflakes that took hours to make, Beth had said, "Oh, don't put those on. They're so old fashioned."

Her mother did not object but simply packed the starched intricate ornaments back in their shoe box. Now, Beth wondered how deeply she had hurt her mother.

She looked through the box and studied each one. They were truly beautiful. But more importantly, her mother had made them lovingly to bring something special to the holiday and the lives of her family.

Nikolai understood this and had appreciated her mother's handiwork from the first day he had come to their home. Beth wondered why she was so rigid on this subject. As an educated woman, she should be able to value whatever a woman chose for her life's work.

Beth jumped up and ran to Nikolai's room. When she knocked on the door, he opened it, holding a notebook.

She spoke quickly. "Nikolai, can you help me?"

"Yes, what must I do?" he said, putting the notebook on a small table by the door.

"We have to go buy another Christmas tree."

"This one is not good?"

"No, it's fine, but I want to put a smaller one in my mother's room."

He nodded. "I will help you."

At the outdoor Christmas tree kiosk, they chose a small tree and brought it home.

After Nikolai set it in the stand, he helped Beth decorate it with the crocheted ornaments and tinsel.

When they finished, she turned to him. "Can you carry the tree into my mother's room?"

Touching one of the starched snowflakes, he looked at Beth and his expression softened. "Of course."

Beth pushed open her mother's door, followed by Nikolai, who carried the tree like a proud standard bearer.

Mrs. Winters asked, "What's going on? I thought you were going to set up the tree in the living room so your friends could see it."

"We set the big one up out there, but I thought you might like a special one in your room."

She felt her eyes fill with tears as her mother's face beamed, and she held out her arms to her daughter. Beth bent down into her mother's embrace, and as the older woman hugged her tightly, Beth whispered, "I'm so sorry that I haven't always appreciated all the wonderful things you do."

"It's all right, my darling," her mother said as she patted her back.

Suddenly, Beth felt the tension that had existed between them fall away. She sat near the bed and held her mother's hand as Nikolai set the tree on a low table. He turned the tree around so they could admire all sides of it.

Beth said, "We need something on the top."

"Isn't there an extra star?" Mrs. Winters asked.

Beth shook her head. "No, we need something that you made." Suddenly Beth jumped up. I know what we can use." She left the room and returned with a fancy red and silver bow attached to a large barrette.

"Mom, do you remember this? You made it for my tenth birthday."

Mrs. Winters studied the bow which she had made with a variety of decorative ribbons and attached it to the barrette. "Beth, you kept this all these years?"

"Yes. It was so beautiful; I saved it in a gift box and put it on the top shelf in my closet when I didn't wear it anymore."

Her mother turned to her. "I never knew that."

Nikolai took the ribbon barrette and fastened it to the top of the tree. "It is just right," he said, smiling.

Mrs. Winters lay her head back on the pillow. "Thank you both for this lovely bit of Christmas."

Beth stood and smoothed her mother's hair. "Mom, you look tired."

"I am. It must be all the excitement of the tree."

Beth leaned down and kissed her mother and whispered, "I love you, Mom."

The older woman placed her hand on her daughter's cheek and said, "I love you too."

Then, Beth led the way out of the room as Nikolai shut the door behind them.

He put his arm around her shoulder. "This may be your mother's last Christmas, but you have made it a very special one."

She leaned her head against his chest and nodded as her eyes misted.

In the kitchen, Beth got ready for her guests. She placed a bottle of wine and five wine glasses on a tray. As she arranged cheese and crackers on a plate, Doreen opened the back door and held it for Amy Ressler and two other language professors.

Doreen hugged her and said, "Hey, girl, how's it going? Is your Mom doing any better on the new medicine?"

Beth smiled. "She's doing okay. Everything's so much better now that I have Nikolai helping me."

"I'm glad the arrangement worked out so well."

Beth chewed on her lip. "Yeah, pretty well."

Doreen checked out the plate of cheese and crackers. "You want me to take this into the living room?"

Beth nodded, and as she picked up the tray with the wine and glasses, she said, "Amy can you get the napkins and small plates?"

Doreen placed the dish on the coffee table, and grabbing a handful of crackers, flopped into an overstuffed armchair, tucking one leg under her. "You have to get out more, Beth. You never go shopping with us or out to eat anymore."

The other women murmured their agreement.

"I have to stay home right now with my mother so sick," Beth said as she poured wine.

One of the women leaned forward in the rocking chair and peered out the window at Nikolai, who was shoveling snow off the sidewalk. "I wouldn't leave the house either if I had a hunk like that guy hanging around. Damn, where'd you get him from? I'd like to know if he's got a brother."

Beth grinned. "Sorry, but he's never mentioned a brother."

Amy followed their gaze. "He's very intelligent, too. I've never seen anyone progress so rapidly. It's amazing how much his English has improved in such a short time. Haven't you noticed it, Beth?"

Beth sat on the sofa and reached for a piece of cheese and a cracker. "Well, he does spend hours at night listening to English tapes, and he reads a lot."

From her seat on the sofa, Beth listened to the soft chatter of her friends and watched Nikolai easily toss a shovelful of snow. His physical strength was evident as she studied his body silhouetted against the darkening snow. But even more formidable was the emotional intensity that blazed in those golden green eyes. They had a way of drawing her in and rendering her helpless.

Beth had always vowed that no man would rule her life. However, she knew instinctively that this man had the potential to do just that. She would have to be more careful around him, and she must keep her head if she was to live the life she wanted.

8

The week before Christmas, Nikolai boasted that he would cook Russian delicacies for the holidays and spent much of his free time shopping with Beth trying to find the specific ingredients he needed.

On Christmas Eve, he shouldered his way through the door of Mrs. Winters' room and set down a tray with three steaming dishes. "I have made you a special supper—stuffed shrimp."

Reaching for her plate, Beth said, "Mmm, it smells good."

But Nikolai put a hand out to stop her. "We must not begin eating until the first star appears in the heavens."

"Why?" asked Beth.

"It is tradition where I come from. This shows respect for the shepherds who followed the star to Bethlehem."

"What a beautiful tradition," Mrs. Winters exclaimed. "We will wait for the star."

Leaning against the window frame, Beth stared out into the blackness of the night and thought of the deeply veiled mystique that shrouded Nikolai. Add that to the handsome face and sculptured body, and you had an almost irresistible combination.

Nikolai came up behind her. Although he did not touch her, the nearness of him and the masculine scent of his aftershave seemed to envelope her. She imagined his arms coming around her possessively as his lips, whispering tender words of love, found the hollow of her neck.

She came out of her reverie when he leaned very close—his lips near her hair—and pointed over her shoulder to a star that had just pierced its way through the black velvet of the sky.

He smiled. "Ah, now we can eat."

All through dinner Beth studied him as he happily entertained her mother with stories of Russia. His easy banter was another characteristic that added to his charm.

On Christmas morning, the three of them congregated in Mrs. Winters' room to open their presents. Nikolai handed out his gifts first. Mrs. Winters opened hers to find a beautiful bright blue woolen shawl with red flowers and green leaves.

"Nikolai, this is lovely. I've never seen anything like it."

"It is a traditional scarf worn by women in Russia, and it is very warm."

Then Beth opened her gift. As the wrappings fell away, she saw a delicate wooden trinket box with a scene painted on the top of it.

"Oh, how beautiful!" she exclaimed.

"This is called a Palekh box because it is hand-painted in a little village of that name. The pictures on top of the boxes are from Russian stories for children." He picked up his dictionary and leafed through it. "Oh, yes, these are called fairy tales."

Studying the painted scene, she asked, "What is this picture of?"

"The story is about a young woman who dreams about Phoenix, the great bird. She asks her father to bring her a feather from this white bird, which is very rare. One day a man gives him a small box, and inside is the feather he needs to make his daughter happy.

"When the daughter is alone in her room, she picks up the feather and lets it fall to floor. It becomes a handsome prince. Instantly, they love each other. Later, he becomes Phoenix again and flies away, but every night he flies to her room and becomes the prince. Servants hear them talking.

"One night, a maid gives the young woman a strong drug for sleep and puts sharp knives on the windowsill. When the bird comes, the girl will not wake up. He is cut by the knives, so he flies away. He thinks the girl does not love him. The father is angry with his daughter when he finds out she has had a man in her room, so he tells her she must leave the house. That night her father dies.

"The daughter wanders around the world looking for her love. She comes to a kingdom and hears that Phoenix, the great bird, has been—how must I say it—burned at the stake because of his magic. The girl cries out for her lost love, 'You are my fate, my love, my all.' When the king sees this, he orders her also to be burned. Soldiers tie her to the stake, but suddenly Phoenix comes alive from the ashes and the girl is on his wings. They fly away, and no one sees them again."

"That is such a sad story until the end," said Beth.

"Sometimes the path to true love is sad," he replied, looking directly at her as he leaned back in his chair and clasped his hands behind his head. Beth gazed at him for a long moment. She was unable to look away until her mother spoke.

"How did you get these gifts?"

"When I talked to my aunt, I told her to send me these things from Russia."

"How is your mother doing?" the older woman asked.

"My mother is not well, but she is taken care of by my aunt."

As he spoke, Beth opened the trinket box. A white feather lay in the bottom. She felt her face flush and her heart beat a little faster as she closed it. When she looked up, Nikolai was talking to her mother but was watching Beth intently.

Beth handed Nikolai gifts from her and her mother. He tore the wrapping paper from one and lifted out a large radio that played CDs. In another box was a stack of compact discs. Nikolai studied the labels of each. Some were Russian classical music, and others were Country Western.

Beth said, "The man at the store told me you could bring back any of the CDs you don't like as long as they're not opened."

"I love all of them," he said, turning them over to read the names of the songs.

"You have one more gift to open. It's from me," said Beth, handing the box to him.

Quickly he removed the paper and found a set of books by James Fenimore Cooper bound in leather. He opened each one and found an inscription, which read, "To Nikolai . . . With Love, Beth." As he looked up from one of the books, his eyes met Beth's igniting a delicious explosion of sparks between them. Beth turned away, pretending to arrange the gifts under the tree.

Nikolai hummed as he prepared a Christmas dinner of roasted chicken, which contained a special bread stuffing. He also made a soup called rassolnik that included chicken and pickled cucumbers. Beth busied herself making potatoes, creamed onions, and gravy. Nikolai carved the chicken while Beth doled out helpings of side dishes for each of them.

Beth set her mother's plate on the tray in front of her and unfolded her napkin for her. Then she and Nikolai took seats with their plates on trays in front of them.

Mrs. Winters asked, "Nikolai, do we have to wait for something before we eat like yesterday?"

He smiled. "No, today we just eat."

While they congratulated Nikolai on his superb dinner, the phone rang. Beth answered it and held the receiver toward Nikolai. "It's for you."

He took the phone and began speaking quietly in Russian.

It was at that moment that Beth decided she would speak to Amy Ressler about learning conversational Russian.

After he hung up, he said, "That was my cousin. Some of our Russian friends are going out tonight. They ask if I want to go with them. I have not seen them for a very long time, so I will go."

Beth had an uneasy feeling about this outing, which she assumed would include Russian women.

"That's wonderful," Mrs. Winters replied. "You're young. You need to get out and have some fun with your friends."

As Nikolai stood in front of his mirror, dressed in his best cashmere sweater and pressed khakis, Beth peeked into the room. "I think your friends are here. There's a black car in the driveway."

Slipping on his jacket, he walked past her in the doorway. She could smell the heavenly scent of his aftershave and desperately wanted to grasp his shoulders and beg him not to go. However, she kept control of herself and said as gaily as possible, "Well, have a good time, but don't drink too much vodka."

Before pulling the front door shut, he grinned. "How can you have a good time without vodka?"

Now it was Beth's turn to pace. She knew Nikolai was attracted to her, but how long would a man stay interested if the object of his affection constantly rebuffed him. He was handsome and charming, and the female population at school found him very attractive. Beth could only assume that Russian women would do the same.

Nikolai and his friends had left quickly, so Beth had not been able to see who was in the black car. She continued to pace as the minutes ticked by. Finally at one o'clock, a car pulled into the driveway.

From her window, she could see Nikolai and a couple of other men get out. The men took turns shaking his hand and clapping him heartily on the back. Then, a blonde woman stepped out. Her open coat revealed a tight dress and a lot of cleavage.

She moved close to Nikolai, and taking his face in her hands, brought his lips to hers. He let her kiss him but made no move to put his arms around her. Then, trying to back away, he was forced to lean down toward her as she continued to press her lips against his. He finally disengaged himself and said his goodbyes to the others as he headed for the house.

Beth jumped into bed, pretending to be asleep as he came down the hall.

In the morning, she dragged herself into the kitchen. As she sat with a cup of coffee, Nikolai came in running a hand through his tousled hair, trying to smooth it.

"How was the party?" Beth asked, stirring the steaming liquid.

"Good, but too much vodka. I have—how do you say it—a hang-over," he said, sitting in a chair.

"So, vodka *can* be a 'dilemma' for Russians."

"This morning, yes . . . it is a dilemma."

Beth got up and opened a bottle of aspirin. She dropped two into her palm and poured a small glass of orange juice. "Here, take these. They might help."

She snapped the cap back on and said, "Was there dancing at the party?"

Popping the aspirins into his mouth, he took a swallow of orange juice.

"Yes," he answered, lolling his head back on his chair.

"What kind of dancing," she asked.

"Some fast and some slow. Like any party."

"Was it at someone's house?"

He rubbed his forehead. "Yes, a friend that I went to school with."

"Male or female?"

"Male," he answered, lifting his head and staring at her.

"After drinking all that vodka, I hope you didn't do anything foolish," she continued as she stirred her coffee.

"What would I do that was foolish?"

"Oh, I don't know, maybe dance around the room with your underwear on your head or have sex with someone you barely know."

"I knew all the women at the party very well," he answered, grinning at her. "And I don't think having sex with the right person is foolish."

"Well, it could be dangerous," she retorted hotly.

"Have you never heard of condoms? If you are worried about my health, I could—how do you say—be monogamous if I got a little—how do you say—cooperation."

Ripples of desire flooded through Beth's body, but she looked away from him as she said, "Well, the only person you looked even remotely monogamous with was that blonde bombshell who got out of the car and attacked you."

"You were watching me? Why?"

"I was worried about you."

He smiled again as he got up and walked past her to put his glass in the sink. "Don't worry. Olga is always very gentle with me."

"That's not the way it looked from my window."

Leaning against the sink, he folded his arms across his chest. "Did you kiss Brad the night he came for you?"

"Yes, I kissed him good night." She stood facing him as she leaned back against the table.

"Then why do you care what I do with Olga?"

"I don't love Brad."

"Do you want me to tell you that I do not love Olga?"

"Do you?" she asked with a piercing look

"No, I don't, but still, she is a temptation," he said, coming near and resting a hand on the table near her.

Beth ran her fingers through her hair, very aware of his closeness. She shook her head in bewilderment. "How do we always end up in these crazy conversations?"

"You asked about the party."

"Okay, okay," she answered.

Nikolai eyed her with a faint smile playing at his lips, and he said, "I think you are jealous."

At that moment, they heard Mrs. Winters calling them. As they entered the room, they found her writhing in pain. Beth rushed to the bedside and shouted to Nikolai to call the doctor.

Dr. Berton, an old friend of Mrs. Winters, came to the house immediately. He was a distinguished looking, portly man with a thin gray mustache and owl-like features. After giving the older woman some pain medication, he, Beth, and Nikolai went into the kitchen to discuss what could be done.

He shook his head. "The cancer is spreading. I think it's time for me to prescribe a morphine patch. It will give her a steady stream of the drug twenty-four hours a day and keep her more comfortable. The patches aren't difficult to apply. I'll have the visiting nurse come out and show you how to do it."

That afternoon with some help from the visiting nurse, Beth and the home health aid learned to apply the morphine patch and within the hour, Mrs. Winters began to feel more comfortable. With the new medication, she slept a lot more. This gave Nikolai more time to work around the house.

One project Beth was concerned about was a clogged gutter which caused long icicles to form. The trouble spot was very high in the eaves, so on the first day warm enough to cause a partial thaw, Nikolai carried the extension ladder from the garage and leaned it against the house, steadying it as well as he could.

Beth stood a small distance away, feeling more and more nervous as she watched him climb higher. She raised her voice so he could hear her. "Nikolai, this is too dangerous. Let's hire someone to do it."

Continuing up the ladder, he called back, "No, no, it will not take me very long."

When he got to the top, Nikolai reached into the gutter and tossed out the debris that blocked the flow of water. Suddenly as he shifted his weight, a stone came loose under one leg of the ladder, and it wobbled dangerously.

Beth darted toward the ladder and leaned against it with all her weight as Nikolai grasped for the gutter. She screamed, "Nikolai, don't fall."

In that instant, she could not imagine her life without him. And with blinding clarity, she knew she loved him.

After clearing away the rest of the debris, Nikolai inched his way down the ladder. At the bottom, he grabbed her by both shoulders. "Why did you come toward the ladder? I could have fallen on you."

She splayed her hands on his chest and cried, "I couldn't let you fall. Soon my mother will be gone, and I can't lose you, too."

He brushed her hair back and looked down into her face. "Do not worry. You will not lose me." Beth caught her breath as he slowly brought his parted lips down to hers.

As their mouths came together in fiery passion, he pulled her close and nudged a thigh between her legs. One hand moved on her back, and the other laced deep in her hair at her neck. Her heart pounded as she reveled in his steamy kisses.

At that moment, from the front of the house, they heard the doorbell ring. A few seconds later, Brad Wilson rounded the corner and headed for the backdoor, carrying a colorfully wrapped Christmas gift. Beth quickly pushed herself away from Nikolai. Straightening her jacket, she smoothed her hair and strode over to greet Brad.

Looking quickly over her shoulder, she saw Nikolai pick up the ladder with a jerk and carry it toward the garage.

On his way to his room, he could hear the professor prattling on about himself. Nikolai closed his door and lay on the bed with his arms bolted across his chest. He was more than just hired help, and she was going to have to face that fact in the very near future.

9

Three days before New Year's Eve, Nikolai knelt on one knee fixing the hinge on a cabinet near the sink while Beth washed dishes. They had said very little to each other since the romantic incident under the ladder and the inopportune appearance of Brad Wilson. All the explosive feelings, the injured pride, and the uncertainty simmered just below the surface.

As Nikolai tightened the last bolt, the phone rang. He put down the screwdriver and stood up to answer it. Disgustedly, he held the receiver toward Beth.

Pulling one hand out of soapy dish water, she took it and said, "Hello? Oh Brad, how are you?"

Nikolai let out an exaggerated sigh.

Beth continued, "Oh, no I can't make it. I'm sorry. No, my mother is far too ill."

As she hung up, Nikolai stared at her.

"New Year's Eve—he wanted to take me out," she said casually.

"And you are not going?"

"No."

"Why not?"

"I don't want to."

Nikolai didn't say anything as he went back to fixing the door.

The next afternoon, Beth was overseeing Nikolai's homework as she prepared sandwiches for lunch. The phone rang and he rose from the table to answer it. Speaking in English, he said, "I would like to come, but I cannot. Have you heard anymore about the appointment? Okay, let me know when it will be."

Once he had hung up, they eyed each other. Finally, Beth said, "You have an appointment? Are you sick?"

"No, no. It is something unimportant."

"Did they invite you out?"

"Yes, for New Year's Eve."

"And you're not going?"

"No, I will spend the night here," he answered as he sat back in a kitchen chair.

Mrs. Winters sat up in her hospital bed, looking perturbed. "Do you mean to tell me that neither of you has a date for New Year's Eve? That's ridiculous. The two of you must go out together."

"Mom, I'll stay here with you," Beth replied.

"Hogwash! Why would you stay home with me? I'm asleep by seven with all the medicine I'm taking. You both deserve a break. Go out somewhere nice."

A little while later, Mrs. Winters dozed off. Beth looked out the window as a thick blanket of snow fell against the dark winter night. Nikolai, apparently lost in thought, sat with one elbow on the arm of the chair and his chin resting on the palm of his semi-closed hand.

Beth asked, "Are you really not going anywhere?"

"No."

"Would you like to go out with me—strictly on a platonic basis, of course."

"Do you know the true meaning of the word platonic? It does not mean friendly. When Plato said it, he meant a great love, but not for a person, for the ideal."

"I think the ideal for us is to go out together on that night and try not to get into an argument or end up wrapped around each other because that only gets us into trouble. Do you think we can handle that?"

"I think so. For that night, I will not argue with you, and I will not wrap myself around you."

"Good. Now try to think of a place where we might go and have some fun."

"I have an idea." He jumped up and ran out to the garage.

Beth waited in the kitchen. After a few minutes he came in, brushing snow off of his sweater and stamping his feet on the rug in front of the door. In his hands, he held a pair of very old ice skates which Beth recognized as her own.

She laughed. "What are you going to do with those?"

"We are going ice skating on New Year's Eve. I must buy myself some, and we will get you a new pair."

On New Year's Eve, Beth watched as Nikolai created a special chicken dish, which he called Kotlety Po-Kievsky. He filled chicken breasts with garlic and butter, rolled them in breadcrumbs and then deep-fried them. As she put the finishing touches on the salad, she asked, "Nikolai, can you get the bottle of champagne in the fridge?"

Beth led the way to Mrs. Winters' room carrying a tray of their plates filled with food, and Nikolai followed holding the bottle by the neck in one hand and three champagne glasses between his fingers in the other.

In Mrs. Winters' room, Nikolai opened the bottle and poured the bubbly liquid into the fluted glasses. He handed each of them a glass and lifted his own.

"What shall we drink to, Nikolai?" Mrs. Winters asked.

He gestured grandiosely toward her. "To a life well lived."

Beth watched as her mother smiled at him and then at her and lifted her glass.

As they all clinked, Beth couldn't help but wonder if Nikolai would think her life was well lived.

Mrs. Winters ate very little and by seven o'clock was dosing. With a neighbor promising to look in on the older woman every hour or so, Beth and Nikolai dressed in sweaters, jeans, and heavy jackets for their night out.

They drove to a large pond on the outskirts of town which was a public skating area. Snow had been cleared off the ice. Music came from large speakers on lighted telephone poles. They put on their skates and held onto each other as they made their way to the ice.

Once there, Beth felt wobbly and unsure of herself, but Nikolai skated around her, smooth as a dancer. He took her hands and skated backward, pulling her along with him. Her hair whipped against her face as they breezed around the pond.

The tempo of the music changed and strains of the song, "Only You" blared from the speakers. Nikolai skated up behind her and wrapped his arms around her waist. He whispered in her ear, "Do not worry that my arms are around you. This is only dancing, not making love. Lean back against my chest."

As she did this, Nikolai glided her across the ice to the beat of the music. Beth nestled deeper into the warmth of his arms. The feel of his breath in her hair sent exquisite shivers of desire racing through her, and she ached for him to touch her intimately. In her desperate need for him, she reached behind her, moving gloved hands with feather lightness on his thighs.

He came to an abrupt stop and turned her around, pulling her close. His dark hair, back-lit from the lights on the poles, shown like an aura as he moved his head down to hers. Then his mouth was on hers. His tongue, hot and demanding, parted her eager lips.

Beth flung her gloved hands around his neck, returning his molten kisses.

He whispered, "Beth, I want you. I love you."

Breathlessly, she asked, "But, Nikolai, how can this work?"

Pressing his lips close to her ear, he said huskily, "We will make it work."

Nikolai and Beth held onto each other as they headed for the car. He said, "Give me the keys. We will go just a short distance up the road." Sitting in the front seat, they quickly took off their skates. He started the engine, then drove up the road, parking in a secluded spot. With his heart pounding, he looked into her eyes as he unzipped her jacket. His hands moved on her back and then found their way under the sweater onto her bare skin. Smoothing his palms over her breasts, he touched them reverently through the bra.

She inhaled sharply as he pulled the bra straps down and ran his thumbs in relentless circles over the nipples.

He stopped his love-making abruptly and said, "We must get into the backseat."

With the car running and the heat on high, the two of them got into the back. They took off their jackets. He pulled off his sweater as she removed her own.

Slowly, Nikolai leaned her back against the leather seat, his hands on her bare shoulders. He brought his head down to hers, kissing her deeply, parting her moist, soft lips with his tongue. Cupping her breasts in his strong hands, his lips skimmed their silky surface. Taking each taut nipple into his mouth, his tongue flicked over each one.

Beth moaned and whispered his name as she ran her fingers through his hair.

He unzipped her jeans, his hands smoothing over her hips as he pushed them down, along with the panties.

He breathed in her ear, "Tell me that you love me, Beth. Just once let me hear you say those words."

Beth moved her head from side to side, almost as a denial of the words she whispered. "I love you. I don't know what's happening to me. I've never fallen in love this way."

Nikolai looked down at her, and in a husky voice, he said, "These many months, I have longed to make such exquisite love to you that you will have no other man."

"You are the only man I want," she murmured as she reached for him.

He took both of her wrists in one hand and held them against the seat above her head as he gazed at her body, beautiful and completely vulnerable. Slowly, he moved the back of his other hand on her skin, trailing from her throat with feather-like lightness to her collarbone and then down across one breast, finally resting at her hip. Then his lips followed, skimming the surface with white-hot sensuousness.

Beth arched her body up toward him, but Nikolai was not going to give her what she wanted just yet. His open wet mouth grazed over her breasts with his tongue darting softly out over the taut dark nipples. Over and over, he tantalized her, savoring the silky warmth of her, but always he moved away at the last moment.

Still holding her hands behind her head with one hand, he fondled her breasts with the other. Then unable to contain his explosive passion, he released her wrists.

Instantly her arms flew around his neck as she returned his scalding kisses. His hands were on her breasts, forcing the nipples to protrude out of his grasp. His mouth frantically covered each dark areola in a desperate effort to possess her completely.

As her hands moved on his back, her every touch was like the heat of a branding iron.

With trembling fingers, Nikolai removed her jeans and panties. He pulled her knee up and kissed her inner thigh as he ran a hand along the length of her leg. Then he moved onto her, her taut nipples pressing against his chest.

His urgent need unleashed, he entered her, moving forcefully. Each thrust catapulted them onto yet a higher level of ecstasy until their bodies shuddered in the throes of an explosively erotic climax. In the afterglow of their lovemaking, they lay entwined in each other's arms as he whispered words of eternal love.

After a while, they dressed leisurely and drove home.

Once inside the door, Nikolai grabbed her arm and pulled her to him. "Sleep with me tonight."

Beth kissed his lips and nodded. "I'll change into my night gown and come to your room."

As Nikolai got into bed, he heard Beth's steps in the hall. She entered the room in a shimmering silk nightgown that encompassed the fullness of her breasts and traced the trimness of her waist. Her hair, normally up, obliterated the thin straps as it flowed in waves around her shoulders

She slipped into bed, and he immediately enfolded her in his arms. Again, he made love to her, and again the wild passion they had for each other mounted out of control and ended with a tenderly passionate climax.

Nikolai awoke in the morning with Beth's back pressed against his chest. Elated that the previous night had not been just another dream, he ran his hands over the silky nightgown that sheathed her body and pulled down the thin straps to massage her breasts. She moved within his arms, but when she reached back to touch his thigh, he could stand it no longer. He turned her toward him, kissing her lips, her neck, and nuzzling his face in her hair.

His hands moved on her waist and hips while his hot, wet mouth found her breasts. As their desire skyrocketed, their bodies melded together in fiery passion that made nuclear fission seem tepid.

In the languid moments after the lovemaking, she leaned on an elbow, hovering above him as he lay on his back and said, "Thank you."

"What are you thanking me for?"

"The pleasure you gave me when we were making love. I didn't think I was capable of feeling that kind of intensity."

As he stroked her body, he gazed up into her eyes. "That is because you have been dating—how do you say—wimps like Brad Wilson."

She laughed. "Well, last night is a night I will always remember."

"You will have this memory and many more with me."

In her own room, Beth showered and wrapped a robe around herself. She sat at the vanity absently brushing her hair as steamy images of their lovemaking waxed and waned in her mind. There was no denying it—she was desperately in love with this man, but some things were going to have to change. She began to work possible solutions out in her head.

When she padded barefoot into the kitchen, Nikolai had already made coffee and was tending a pan of eggs. As she brushed past him to get the orange juice out of the refrigerator, he scooped an arm around her, pulling her close and nuzzling his face in her hair. Putting her head back leisurely, she allowed him to kiss her neck.

She moved away from him to get a glass. "Nikolai, I've been thinking. We need to get you into a full-time schedule at the university. Then once you have a degree, you can find yourself a good job."

"I like this job," he said in a flat voice, turning his head away from her.

"Come on. You can't be serious. With your intelligence you can get a good position. All you have to do is get through the university."

"That is not what I want," he replied tersely.

"Well, what do you want?"

"I told you, I want to remain at this job."

"Listen, let's get you matriculated into the college full-time, and when you're through, if you still want this job, we'll talk about it."

"No!" he said more firmly.

"What the hell is wrong with you? You took one class and aced it, so what are you worried about?"

"Why can't you accept me as I am?" He turned off the stove with a jerk and threw the spatula into the sink. "Must I be some professor or bank manager for you to love me? Why are you ashamed of a man who works with his hands?"

Beth sank into a kitchen chair. "I just don't understand why you don't want to try for a better life."

He came to her and going down on one knee, he pushed her hair back. "Right now, I cannot."

She put her hands on the sides of his face and studying his eyes, asked, "Why?"

He took a deep breath and leveled his gaze to hers. "I am not legal in this country. I have no passport or visa to travel here, and I have no social security number. To go to the university full-time, I would have to have a student visa and a social security number."

"You're not legal?"

"No," Nikolai said, turning his head away.

"I don't understand. Are you the same status as a migrant worker?" she asked, almost grimacing.

"Unfortunately, no. They are legal when they are working in this country. If authorities found me, I would be deported back to Russia."

"How did you get here?"

"It is a long story."

"Well, how can we make you legal?" she asked.

Not meeting her gaze, he said, "I will talk to someone who knows."

He put his arms around her waist. Gently, he pressed his head against hers. "Do not worry, my love. It will be all right. I will call a friend today who might know about these things."

10

Beth went in to check on her mother and pulled the blanket up over her sleeping figure, then went into her room. Nikolai's words played over and over in her mind as she dressed in jeans and a sweater.

With her brows knit together, she chewed on her lip. *The only person who might be able to straighten this out is a lawyer.* She slipped into the library and closed the door. Leafing through her Rolodex, she found the home phone number of her attorney, Jim Atkins.

When he answered the phone, Beth said, "Hi, Jim, it's Beth Winters. Do you have a minute? I have a small problem."

"Sure, shoot."

After telling him about Nikolai's situation, she added, "I had no idea he was illegal."

"Well, you know, Beth, these people really don't advertise the fact because if they are forced to leave this country, their chances of coming back are slim, and the economy over there is in shambles."

She asked, "How can we make him legal?"

"The only sure thing is to try to marry him off to an American. That works, but he has to be married for five years, and he must live with the woman. Immigration can be pretty sticky about it, and they will check up on the couple to make sure they are living as husband

and wife. It's a big inconvenience, but there are people out there who will marry illegal aliens for a price. It might be better just to leave well enough alone because as long as he doesn't break the law, he probably won't be found out."

Beth hung up the phone and went to Nikolai's room. He was lying on the bed dressed in blue jeans and an open flannel shirt with his hands behind his head. As she entered, he turned to look at her.

Her glance took in his muscled torso and the bed where they had spent the night in sensual intimacy. She wanted to rush to him and put her arms around him, telling him everything would be all right, but *would* everything be all right?

He got up and came over to her. Putting his hands on her upper arms, he pleaded, "I love you, Beth. I need you. Why must things change? We can be happy the way we are."

Making no move to touch him, she stared up at him. "Did you know that marrying an American citizen would make you legal?"

He sighed deeply. "Yes."

"Then how can I tell if you really love me or if you're just trying to get citizenship?"

"You cannot tell that I love you when I touch you?"

"It seems like you do, but men are different than women. A man can make love to a prostitute just as well as his wife."

"I have not been with another woman since the first day we met. And I could have. Remember Olga? She wanted me to sleep with her, but I already was in love with you, and I could not betray those feelings."

"I'm so confused," she answered, looking away from him.

His eyes blazed with fiery intensity. "You can be sure of this. I will love you forever."

"I don't feel sure of anything."

He gripped her arms. "I was not the one who asked for citizenship. I was happy working here and loving you. You are the one who insisted that I must go to school to find a better job, so why are you accusing me of anything?"

"Oh, Nikolai, I just don't know what to think."

Putting his arms around her, he said, "Lie down with me on my bed, and you will have no doubts about my love."

"I can't . . . I just can't. I won't be used, and I don't have five years to throw away on a marriage that might end with citizenship papers."

Nikolai gripped her arms tighter and hissed, "How can you turn your love off and on like an American faucet?" He released his hold on her abruptly and quickly buttoned the flannel shirt. Then he put on his jacket and stalked out of the house.

Beth was beside herself with worry and fear. What if he didn't come back? Would she lose him forever because she couldn't get past this issue? And she also feared he would now go to the arms of Olga to get what she, herself, refused to give him.

Beth began to pace. Every few minutes she pulled the curtain aside, hoping to see him coming up the walk. At ten o'clock, she couldn't stand the suspense any longer. She called Doreen Johnson and asked for the Russian cleaning woman's number. Holding her breath, Beth punched in the number.

"Hello," said a man with a thick Russian accent.

Beth cleared her throat. "This is Beth Winters calling. I was wondering if Nikolai Mendeleyev is there."

"He is here," answered the man.

"Could I please speak to him?"

She could hear the man talking with someone who sounded like Nikolai. Finally, his familiar voice came over the line. "What do you want from me?"

In a tumble of words, Beth cried, "Nikolai, I was wrong to make such an issue of this whole thing, but I've never been so torn in my life. I love you desperately. I've never said that to a man before. If I mean anything at all to you, please come back."

"I only meant to stay away until tomorrow, but I will come back tonight," he said. He breathed deeply into the receiver. "I only wish I could make you feel how deep my love for you is."

Feeling tears just below the surface, she said, "Come back, Nikolai."

As Sergei's black car pulled into the Winters' driveway, Nikolai could see the flashing lights of an ambulance. Quickly pushing open the car door, he said, "Something must have happened to Mrs. Winters."

His cousin grabbed his arm. "Do not forget our appointment. Make sure you have that night off."

"Okay, okay," he said, getting out of the car and rushing toward the house. Inside he found two EMTs hooking up oxygen tanks by Mrs. Winters' bed.

He stopped one of the attendants. "What has happened?"

"Mrs. Winters was having trouble breathing, but she's more comfortable now."

"Where is her daughter?" said Nikolai.

"She felt faint, so we helped her into her room."

Nikolai rushed down the hallway to her room. She was sitting on the bed with her head in her hands.

When he spoke her name, she flew into his arms. "Thank God you're here. Right after I talked to you, I went in to check on my mother, and her breathing was very labored, so I dialed 911 and called Dr. Berton. He should be here any minute."

"The attendant says she is comfortable now. You are all right?" he asked.

"Now that you're here, I'll be okay." She buried her face in his chest.

Rocking her gently, he rested his chin on the top of her head. "Beth, I have been thinking about all of this unhappiness that we are causing each other. We will not deal with this now. When your mother is gone, then we will decide what kind of relationship we want."

"All right, Nikolai," she answered as she leaned her head against him.

At the sound of the doorbell, they moved away from each other. Beth hurried into the foyer and let Dr. Berton into the house. She led the way into the sick room where the EMTs were just finishing up.

The doctor examined the older woman who was now draped with oxygen paraphernalia. Then he put his stethoscope into his bag and patted Mrs. Winters' hand. "Just rest easy, and you should be feeling better in a bit."

He and Beth stepped into the hall to discuss medical options while Nikolai sat by Mrs. Winters' bed.

The older woman looked up at him and said in a faint voice, "My time is near, Nikolai, and honestly, I'm afraid to die."

"Do not be afraid to leave your earthly body behind. Your journey is to a place where your soul began. It is a serene place which is the soul's true home. I will miss you though because I feel as if you are a mother to me."

The older woman's eyes softened. "But you have your own mother."

"My mother's life was dancing in the ballet, but once she gave birth to my sister and me, she had to retire from that which was her first love. She never forgave either of us for that."

"How terrible that she never realized what a wonderful son she has. I have treasured your company these last few months." She placed her hand over his and closed her eyes. When she opened them again, she said, "Nikolai, I must ask one thing of you."

"Anything, dear lady."

"Promise me that you will take care of Beth when I'm gone."

"That is not an easy thing to do. Beth will not believe that I love her, and her mind rules her heart."

Mrs. Winters stopped talking and rested a moment, then continued, "Believe me, Nikolai, she is not as tough as she appears to be. She feels she must be strong and capable, but underneath she is unsure of herself. She needs your strength."

"As long as it is possible for me, I will be here for her."

The next day, Beth tried to feed her mother clear broth, but she could sip only small amounts and spoke very little, conserving her breath.

In the evening, as her mother dozed, Beth slipped her jacket on and went outside into the clear cold night air, trying to escape the antiseptic smell of the sick room. She pulled the outer garment more closely around her, remembering it was inside this jacket that Nikolai had put his hands to touch her body.

A warm fuzzy feeling enveloped her as she thought of their love-making and the passion they had experienced in each other's arms. It was all so beautifully intoxicating until reality, with all its uncertainties, undermined their love.

As Beth looked up at the brilliant star-studded sky, she heard a noise in the garage. Nikolai stepped out of the inky darkness of the evergreens and walked up the sidewalk.

He came up close behind her. "Do you know the stars?"

"A few," she answered, turning her head to look back at him.

He put his hand on her right shoulder and pointed with his other hand over her left shoulder. "Do you know what that large star is?"

"No," she answered as instant fiery tingles flooded her body.

"That is Venus. Galileo called this planet the mother of love. Then he pointed to another place in the sky. "See Ursa Major?"

"We call it the Big Dipper," she said.

He continued, "And there is Ursa Minor with Polaris at the end of it."

"Polaris is the North Star, isn't it?"

"Yes. It is one of the few objects that does not change its place in this changing universe. The poles melt, cities fall to the ground, volcanoes put what is inside the earth on the outside, and even the sand on beaches leaves one shore and is washed to another, but Polaris can always be found in its place in the sky."

He brought his chin down close to her shoulder. "The ancient Greeks thought that the stars were alive—perfect living bodies in space, which moved in their own order. And, it is true. They always follow the path of least resistance. Unlike people, the stars do not struggle against their destiny."

"For most of us, the path is not that easy," Beth said as she turned her head to look over her shoulder at him. "And sometimes it is downright impossible."

Resting his elbows on the outside edge of her shoulders, he crossed his arms in front of her and placed his hands on her collarbones, massaging the area lightly with his fingertips.

Then, gently easing her back against his chest, he said, "Galileo believed that our lifetime on Earth, whether it is good or bad, is a gift from God and that the bad things are necessary to make a person more spiritual."

"Well, that philosophy isn't working for me."

"Maybe the difficulty is all in your own head."

Looking up at the stars again, she answered, "As a woman in control of my own destiny, I must live by the rules I set for myself. How can I just abandon everything I've lived by for a lifetime?"

"Our time on Earth is so short compared to the eternity of the universe. Why not just listen to your heart?"

"My pride won't allow it."

"The Bible says that pride is a sin. And pride is not always a good thing. What if, because of it, you someday find yourself an old woman without children and without a man to love you? How would you feel then?"

"I don't know," she answered, looking up at him again.

"Remember this, as a woman, your most important purpose in this universe—the reason you were created—is to yield your body to a man you love, to carry his seed in your belly and to nurse his children at your breast. Without this, there would be no human race."

"Nikolai, we're living in the twenty-first century. Women may have higher goals in life than just getting married and having children."

"They may do other things—yes—but without a man and children, a woman's true destiny is not fulfilled."

Keeping her back to him, she said with gentle resignation, "Why must you win every argument?"

"Because I also am guilty of pride."

She sighed. "How can two proud people come to terms with each other in this world?"

Turning her around, he slipped an arm around her shoulder and led her toward the house. "We will find that out after your mother's difficult illness is over. Come, I will make you some hot chocolate."

Beth leaned her head against his chest, taking in the masculine scent of his cologne, and let him walk her into the house.

Nikolai stood at the stove, stirring cocoa into milk while she sat at the table. Topping the steaming mug with whipped cream, he set it in front of her. Like a child, she hovered over the cup, enjoying the rich aroma of chocolate.

The phone rang, and Nikolai reached for it. He studied her as the hushed voice of Sergei came through the receiver. Speaking rapidly in Russian, he said. "Tomorrow night I will pick you up at 10:00, and we will try again."

Nikolai's glance lingered on Beth. "Why didn't you tell me sooner?"

"I just found out myself."

Nikolai sighed. "I will be ready."

11

Nikolai helped Beth with the supper dishes the next evening. He folded the small towel and placed it on the counter. "I must do some homework. I will be in my room if you need me."

In reality, he had none, but being near her caused him to rethink these dangerous outings with Sergei. He lay on his bed with his arm across his eyes. He knew if he were caught, he would never see her again.

Nikolai checked his clock—10:00 flashed on the screen. He pulled on his jacket and headed for the kitchen. He found Beth sitting at the table stirring sugar into her tea.

Walking toward the door, he zipped his jacket.

"Are you going somewhere?" she asked.

"Yes, I must go out."

"So late, Nikolai?"

"Some business does not wait," he said, smiling as he opened the back door.

Lighting a cigarette, he walked quickly down the driveway. Sergei's black car rolled to a stop, and Nikolai opened the door and swung into the seat. Exhaling smoke, he said, "I hope this trip will be less eventful than the last."

Sergei checked his mirror for traffic and pulled away from the curb. "Unfortunately, we have no choice if we want a chance to live the American good life."

Nikolai nodded but wondered if his life would ever be good if Beth wasn't a part of it.

They spoke little for most of the trip, but as they drove down the dark streets near the docks of New York, Sergei handed Nikolai a crudely drawn road map.

"We are here," Sergei said, thrusting his index finger at one spot on the map. "And if we follow this road along the water, we should come to the building soon."

Suddenly, Nikolai pointed at a structure that appeared to be an abandoned warehouse. "This must be the place."

The old brick building stood by itself near the wharf. Again, the windows were painted black with a faint glimmer of light coming through. Next to the building was a parking lot enclosed by a chain link fence.

Sergei headed for the lot, but Nikolai said, "No, don't park there. Park here on the street. We can walk."

Sergei pulled over and looked at Nikolai. "Do you think this is a good idea? What if someone steals the car?"

Nikolai rubbed his chin. "It is better not to be trapped inside that fence."

As he reached for the door handle, he glanced in the outside mirror. Hairs prickled on the back of his neck as he spotted a fleet of silent police cars with lights flashing slowly cruise toward the building. He jutted a finger in the direction of the police and hissed, "Let's get out of here."

Keeping their lights off, Sergei made a quick U-turn and sped away. "That was close," Sergei said as he wiped nervous sweat from his forehead.

Nikolai shook his head. "Getting these false papers appears to be more difficult than we expected."

Sergei grunted in assent. "I am told that the police are even using our own people as informants."

Nikolai pulled a pack of cigarettes from his shirt pocket and tapped one out. "We are caught in a very dangerous business," he said, looking out the window but thinking of Beth.

Beth found the private classes in conversational Russian to be more difficult than she had anticipated. As she and Nikolai sat in her mother's room every night, he helped her with word pronunciation and sentence construction. In addition to learning the language, she began reading some Russian history and literature.

One evening as she opened a book of Pushkin's poetry, Nikolai took it out of her hands and thumbed through it.

"You know that Pushkin is the most important Russian poet," he said, studying the cover.

"No, I didn't. I really have never read anything of his."

"Did you know that his great grandfather was an African slave?"

"No."

"Yes, he was the son of an Abyssinian prince. After his father was defeated in a war with the Turks, the boy was abducted and eventually was brought to the court of Peter the Great, who became fond of him. He educated the boy, and as a grown man, his technical ability was so great that he was made chief of the Russian Engineer Corps."

"That's an unbelievable story," Beth said. "So, the poet Pushkin is the great grandson of that man?"

"Yes."

"It says in the prologue of this book that he died at the age of thirty-six."

"That is true," answered Nikolai. "He was shot in the stomach during a duel with a French military officer named D'Anthes."

"Why?"

Nikolai's eyes sparkled with intrigue. "Not only did this man insult Pushkin's poetry, but he also was desperately in love with Pushkin's wife."

Reaching across Beth's seated figure, Nikolai's arm almost brushed her midsection as he grasped a book that lay on the table just beyond her chair. "Ah . . ." he said, "another great poet, Marina Tsvetaeva who, like so many others, would not bow down to authority and because of this, experienced exile and tragedy."

"What happened to her?" Beth asked.

"In the end, she killed herself."

"How do you know all this?"

He shrugged. "I like to read about these things."

"Did you go to a university in your country?"

"No, there was no money for that."

Beth sighed. "So many people lead such unhappy lives. Even for you it must be hard so far from your homeland and family. I can't imagine how many other people are living in this country illegally and never see their families."

"There are many. They must stay and work because their families cannot survive without the money they send."

"It's sad, though. How long has it been since you last saw your mother?"

"About a year, but that is not as bad as some," he replied as he leaned back in his chair and locked his hands behind his head. "I know woman who has been working here for four years. She has a husband and five-year old daughter who she has not seen since she was a baby. And a man from Cambodia told me he waited fourteen years before he could get his wife and children here."

"That's so terrible. How do they stand it?"

"In this life we must do what we can. After a few years, out of sadness and loneliness, many find another person to fill the wife's or husband's place. Some of these people have been together longer here than they were with their husbands or wives over there."

"Do you have a wife in Russia?" she asked.

He smiled reassuringly. "No. It is all I can do to take care of my mother."

"You would tell me, wouldn't you?"

"Of course, I could not lie about something like that."

She chewed her lip. *Well, there was the lie of omission, concerning his legality in this country.*

12

In the weeks that followed, Mrs. Winters' condition took a dramatic downturn. As Beth and Nikolai kept watch at the sick bed, they could see the older woman's breathing become more labored even with the oxygen, and she barely sipped water. Day by day, the light in her bright blue eyes faded.

The round-the-clock care and terrible sadness left Beth and Nikolai too exhausted to deal with the problems of their relationship, but still when their eyes met, they brimmed with their longing and desire.

One morning as Nikolai's all-night vigil ended, he touched the older woman's hand. It was warm, but she did not respond. He rushed to Beth's room. "Beth, we must call the doctor. Your mother will not wake."

Dr. Berton came out to the house. After examining Mrs. Winters, he said, "There isn't anything more we can do. Now, it's just a matter of time."

Beth sat heavily in a chair and covered her face. Nikolai stood behind her with his hands on her shoulders.

On a cold snowy evening in February, Mrs. Winters died peacefully.

Nikolai sat with Beth on her bed, holding her close and whispering words of comfort. "Beth, death is only so terrible and final on this mortal side of it. Remember the day we talked about evolution? It happens also with the spirit. When we have become the most spiritual, then we have completely evolved, and I believe your mother was at that place."

Beth pressed her head against his chest. "I hope so, Nikolai."

At her mother's wake, Beth stood in the receiving line. Across the room, she saw groups of people talking, some even laughing. There were friends, colleagues, and a few distant cousins. *Everyone has someone but me*, she thought. Only Nikolai looked as lonely and sad as she did, his dark brooding eyes fixed on her mother's casket.

Beth sat in the chair, looking at the mahogany coffin with its huge spray of red roses and thought, *What will become of me?* She had some close friends, but they all had their own families. Her closest relatives were second cousins who lived in another part of the state. They came today to pay their respects, but she knew that it would only be at the next funeral in the family that she would see them again.

The air, permeated with the scent of roses and gardenias, engulfed her, almost suffocating her. Only Nikolai, sitting so near, kept her tethered to her surroundings, but how long would he stay if she continued to focus on all the uncertainties of their relationship?

A blustery wind whipped through the tent at the cemetery. Nikolai stood behind Beth, who was seated. She could feel his hands against her back as they rested on the canvas chair and felt comforted by even that slight touch.

The service ended, and people walked toward their cars. As Beth stood over the casket, a man from the funeral home gave her a rose from a bouquet. Suddenly, in a spinning haze, the world went pale and Beth faltered. Nikolai rushed to her side. His quiet voice was anxious. "Beth, are you all right?"

"I'm okay—just a little dizzy."

"Here, lean on me."

As he supported her, she leaned against his chest, her eyes stinging with hot tears.

Pulling her close, he whispered in her ear, "It will be all right. We will take care of each other."

In the days that followed the funeral, Beth wandered from room to room, trying to find a spot where she might feel comfortable, but her grief and worries about the future kept any kind of physical or emotional comfort from her.

When she looked at Nikolai, she knew he was suffering, too. For now, they must comfort each other and then, later, confront the troubling issues of their relationship.

From Nikolai's room, she could hear the sounds of mournful country music. The soft voices and poignant words seemed to soothe him, and in a way they soothed her, too.

March's brisk winds blew through the house, helping to dislodge the preoccupation with death that dwelled there, and the golden peach-colored light of spring settled in Beth's kitchen, bringing with it a budding feeling of hope.

One Saturday morning as she brought out the trash, she saw Nikolai raking up all the dead leaves and plants in one of her mother's perennial gardens.

It seemed a symbolic gesture to Beth, and she rushed over to him. "Nikolai, let's buy pansies, lots of them, so the garden will be colorful until the perennials start to bloom."

Setting the rake down, he put an arm around her shoulder and said, "Yes, we will go now."

As they perused the aisles of pansies at the local garden center, Beth said, "My mother's favorite color was yellow."

"Then, we will buy yellow flowers. And you, what is your favorite color?"

"In pansies, I think purple."

"Good, and we will get some blue ones for me."

"Yes, they'll kind of fit our mood," Beth said with a wan smile.

Beth watched Nikolai turning over the moist dark earth streaked with bright sunlight and got down on her knees near him to help plant the pansies.

As they put in the last of the flowers, Nikolai stuck the shovel into the soil. He squatted down beside her, one knee touching the ground, and grasped the lower part of the handle to steady himself. He gazed at the window of Mrs. Winters' bedroom and suddenly his eyes filled with tears.

Beth pulled off her planting gloves and placed her hand on his shoulder. He turned his head to kiss her fingertips where they lay. Watching him, she felt as if her heart would break.

His arm came around her in a gentle embrace. Ah, to stay like this forever, enveloped in his strength and warmth, banishing from her consciousness the questions that plagued her.

He brushed a featherlight kiss on her forehead. Then, his eyes impaling hers, he brought his lips down so close to hers—those soft full lips.

But feeling tears come, she looked away. How could she ever be content not knowing the truth about his feelings?

The next morning, Beth brought in the mail and noticed a letter for Nikolai. As he came into the kitchen, buttoning the cuff of his shirt, she said, "Something for you from Russia."

He tore the envelope open and read the contents of the letter. He lay the paper down on the table and ran his fingers through his hair.

"What is it?" she asked.

"I must go back to Russia."

"Why? What's the matter?"

"It is my mother. She is very close to death, and she wants to see me."

"Will you be able to come back here?"

"No."

"How can you be so sure?" she replied, cold fear gripping her.

"Once the authorities know I am there, they will arrest me."

"Why? Are you a criminal?"

"To them, yes, I am."

"What was your crime?"

"It was a political offense against the state."

"I thought the government in Russia was all washed up."

"There is still the KGB. It may have a new name, but it has the same agents. And they do not forget."

"What'll they do to you?"

He sat back in his chair and looked past her out the window. "I will be sent to a prison camp in Siberia."

"Oh, my God! Is there any way to keep that from happening?"

"Yes."

"What is it?"

"I must be an American citizen."

"According to my lawyer, the only way that's going to happen is if you marry an American."

"Yes," he answered, looking ashamed. He got up and leaned against the counter, staring out the window.

Beth didn't speak for a long time. Finally, she said, "Why do you have to go back? My mother told me there was almost no affection between you and your mother."

"She is still my mother, and it is her dying wish to see me one last time."

Beth's mind raced. She could not let him be arrested. She knew that for him to be legal in this country, they would have to be married for five years. But, maybe, to get him in and out of Russia safely, it could just be for a short amount of time.

She turned to him. "Okay, then, let's do this. You and I will get married, and I will go with you to Russia. But, please, Nikolai, this is a marriage in name only. Can you accept that?"

"Yes," He said, looking down.

13

To keep immigration happy, Beth and Nikolai had decided on a small church wedding with Doreen Johnson as matron of honor and Nikolai's cousin Sergei as best man.

Looking in his mirror, Nikolai worked at fastening the top button of his starched white shirt. Then he put on the black and white pin-striped tie. As he smoothed it down inside the jacket of his new black suit, he studied his appearance. Would Beth find him a presentable husband on this, their wedding day?

Nikolai heard Beth's steps in the hall. She stopped at his door and peeked in. How exquisite she looked in the cream-colored silk dress with the silk-fringed shawl. A five-inch slit at the hem of the calf-length skirt accentuated her shapely legs. Her hair, adorned with a sweet smelling gardenia, was put up in the Gibson-girl-style that she always wore.

To Nikolai, she looked as beautiful as the night she had gone to the play with Brad Wilson. But, he knew that the kiss Brad had gotten that evening was far more passionate than any he would be getting from her tonight.

Would this marriage of convenience ever become anything more? He guessed not unless he could prove to Beth that his love was true.

They met the few invited friends and relatives at the small steepled, whitechurch and went inside. Sergei, a stocky man with a broad face and clear blue eyes, put a beefy hand on Nikolai's shoulder.

Beth waited at one end of the vestibule as the guests entered the church. When Doreen came in, she caught Beth's eye and blew her a kiss. After everyone was seated, the "Wedding March" began. Beth, carrying a bouquet of pink oriental lilies, walked toward the altar, which was decorated with vases of white long-stemmed roses and lighted cream-colored candles.

The friends they had invited sat in groups in the front pews on either side of the aisle. Beth stared down at her bouquet until she reached Nikolai's side, and with myriad butterflies creating havoc in her stomach, she took his hand.

The priest began the ceremony, and Beth looked straight ahead, trying to appear in control of her emotions, but her heart fluttered in her chest like the last desperate flight of a dying bird caught in a cage. When she said, "I will," tears spilled over her lashes. *Why couldn't this marriage be something other than the sham it is?*

As Nikolai said his vows to Beth, he stared into her eyes, appearing to mean every word.

The short service ended with the minister saying, "I now pronounce you man and wife." He looked at Nikolai. "You may kiss your bride."

Nikolai pulled Beth close and his kiss was deep and sensual enough to convince any immigration officer who might be lurking somewhere in the church that their commitment to each other was real. As his hands moved on her back, she could feel their warmth through the silk.

When the kiss ended, Beth moved back breathlessly from his grasp. His hands smoothed around, high up on her sides, and his thumbs moved along the underside of her breasts. Fiery shivers shot through her. She wondered if the touch could be accidental or if Nikolai meant to drive her crazy.

The small entourage had dinner in a private room at Nistico's Restaurant. A string quartet played softly as the meal of stuffed chicken was served. After dinner, Beth and Doreen met in the ladies' room.

Doreen hugged her, staring into her face. "Are you all right?"

Beth stepped back and placed one hand on the sink and the other against her mid section. "Yeah, I'm okay."

"How are you going to handle this trip?"

Beth shrugged. "Doreen, I have to do this."

Doreen shook her head. "Well, just try to relax, and who knows, you might even enjoy it."

Doreen put an arm around Beth's waist and walked Beth back into the banquet room. Nikolai motioned for her to join him. They stood in front of the three-tiered cake, edged with decorative rosebuds, and together they sliced the first piece.

As coffee and cake were served, Nikolai and Beth went from table to table thanking their guests for coming. Beth's friends hugged her and shook Nikolai's hand warmly. Sergei and Tania kissed them on both cheeks and wished them a safe journey.

After the guests had left, Nikolai and Beth collected their gifts and made their way to the car. On the silent drive home, Beth wondered what the future would bring.

At home, they checked their luggage which was packed for the next day's trip to St. Petersburg. All their papers and money for the trip were in small carrying cases made to hang from the shoulder.

Beth went into the bedroom to change into a nightgown and robe. When she came out, she left the door open for him to go in. All of his clothes were in her room in case of a surprise visit from immigration. He would also be sleeping in there tonight for the same reason.

Dressed only in pajama bottoms, Nikolai lay down on folded quilts on the floor, wedging a pillow behind his head.

Beth removed her robe and slipped into bed. Looking down at him, she said quietly, "Nikolai, if you want, you can sleep in the bed. You need to get your rest for the trip tomorrow."

"The floor is good," he answered, rolling up in the blankets.

"The bed is so big, we'll never touch each other all night."

"Do not worry about me. I am fine."

At six o'clock the next morning, they were on an Aeroflot flight to Helsinki, which would then go on to Pulkovo 2 in St. Petersburg. Although Beth held her breath going through customs, the official stamped Nikolai's documents without incident.

They emerged from the airport into a light rain. Beth noticed a man leaning against a car and waving to them.

Nikolai called out a joyous greeting in Russian as he pulled his suitcase to the car; the two men bear-hugged and exchanged affectionate greetings.

Beth rolled her suitcase up to Nikolai's. He turned to her and introduced his friend. As the man greeted Beth with a warm handshake and a kiss on both cheeks, she studied him. Dmitri was a heavyset man with thin lips and a neatly clipped mustache. A small, flat, black cap with a narrow visor hooded his dark piercing eyes.

Turning to Nikolai, he put a hand on his shoulder and said in English, "I am sorry to have to tell you this unfortunate news, but your mother died early this morning."

Nikolai shook his head. "Even in her last moments, my mother has kept herself from me."

As they loaded the luggage into Dmitri's car, he added, "The house was closed up, but when I heard you were coming, I had Anna and her husband come back and get it ready for you."

When they came to an area known as the English Quay, they drove down a side street and entered the driveway of a secluded estate which was lined with high cement walls overgrown with thick vines. Near the end of the driveway, a large house came into view.

The style was very quaint with a steeply pitched slate roof. On the left side rose a stone turret. Hooded dormers jutted out across the main roof ending with a high chimney at the far right. Other chimneys rose from the back of the house. Willowy trees, shrouded in a misty twilight rain, arced gracefully against the house.

The car pulled up to the entrance, and a woman and man in servants' uniforms came out. Beth looked at Nikolai, wondering who these people were and whose house this was.

The older couple walked to the car. The man named Derrick grasped Nikolai's hand warmly. He was short and heavyset, and Beth couldn't help but think his bushy eyebrows and mischievous light blue eyes reminded her of one of the seven dwarfs.

The woman, who Nikolai addressed as Anna, wore her gray hair in braids that wound into a bun on top of her head. Dressed in black with a white starched apron around her ample middle, she patted him on the back in a motherly fashion.

Anna opened an umbrella and held it over Beth as she got out. Together, they walked up the steps to the stone landing. As Anna opened the door, Beth noticed the large door knocker, which appeared to be a brass coat of arms.

They entered an elegant foyer, brightly lit by an antique crystal chandelier that hung high above their heads. The floor was covered with large green and white marble squares. To the left, a grand staircase with a banister of intricately carved spindles led to the second floor. Here, this ornate railing turned sharply to the right, following the open balcony along the second floor hall.

To the right of the foyer, a rounded archway opened into a sprawling formal parlor with tufted velvet high-backed sofas and chairs and highly polished tables. A wide hall at the back of the foyer led to rooms beyond.

After Derrick and Anna took the bags upstairs, Beth roamed through the parlor. She pushed open French doors that led into a large dining room. This room also was lit with a glittering crystal chandelier. She marveled at the antique baroque dining room table with tufted armchairs and matching sideboard.

A massive hutch of dark wood stood against one wall. Its upper cupboard doors shone with antique panes of beveled glass. An ornate set of hand painted china was displayed within. Large oil paintings in heavy gilded frames adorned the walls.

In the back of the house was a large kitchen with a white tiled floor. Blue and white tiles decorated the walls and heavy cotton lace curtains covered the windows. A round wooden table with chairs stood in the center of the room.

Beth noticed what appeared to be an odd-shaped antique coffee urn set on a small table in a corner of the room. It looked as if it were gold-plated and had an ornate spout as well as intricately carved wooden handles and an elaborately worked pedestal. At the top, in the center, was a cylindrical opening. When she peered down into it, she found it extended deep into the middle of the pot. Since the urn was not electrified, Beth assumed it was somehow heated from this center.

She returned to the foyer to find Anna coming down the stairs. Nikolai spoke to the woman in an authoritative manner as if he had commanded servants all his life. Beth followed them with her eyes as they headed for the kitchen. Gone was the man who had stood before her respectfully while she told him what his jobs for the day were.

When he reentered the room, she said, "Nikolai, I don't understand . . . this house, the servants . . ."

"Beth, you look tired. Let me show you to your bedroom."

As they started up the stairs, Dmitri began to speak, but Nikolai cut him off.

From what she had learned in Amy Ressler's class, Beth thought she heard Nikolai say, "The woman knows a little of our language, so be careful what you say."

Still wondering what Nikolai didn't want her to hear, Beth followed him into an enormous bedroom with high ceilings, massive baroque furniture and heavy velvet drapes tied back with tasseled cording. The huge bed was made of grandly ornate wrought iron, and the spread was also of velvet. Thick oriental carpets lay across the floor.

Feeling bewildered, Beth looked at Nikolai. "What are we doing here? Who owns this house?"

Nikolai turned down the bed for her. "Do not worry about these things tonight. We will talk in the morning."

Nikolai met Dmitri in the kitchen. They pushed open the back door and followed a cobblestone walk which led to a small guesthouse at the back of the property. Stepping inside the cottage with its lace veiled windows and dark furniture, Nikolai greeted his aunt with a hug. Dmitri waited in the doorway as the aunt led Nikolai to the bedroom, where the body of his mother lay with her hands crossed at her chest.

No tears stung his eyes. In death, just as in life, his mother was remote and unapproachable. He went close to the bed and looked down at her. He had not remembered her hair so gray and her body so thin.

His aunt laid a comforting hand on his arm. "My friends at the funerary establishment agreed not to come for your mother until you had seen her."

The older woman didn't speak for a moment; then she continued, "I know she was not a very good mother to you and Amalia. I hope you can forgive her."

He kept his gaze on his mother. "I accepted the situation a long time ago."

"That is good. And now, you must go on with your own life. Who is the woman you have brought with you?"

"My wife."

"When did you wed? We heard nothing about it."

"Just before we came here. We only married so that I could come here without being arrested."

"So, there is no love between you?"

Nikolai sighed. "I love her."

"Does she love you?"

"Yes, but there are problems."

"Between a man and a woman there always are." She patted Nikolai's arm. Then, she turned and laid her hand over the dead woman's. "For over a year, I have been caring for her. I will miss her."

Nikolai put his arm around his aunt. "I thank you for all you have done."

She nodded solemnly. After a moment, she said, "I have kept your mother's death quiet. We don't want any officials snooping around here. Does anyone know you're here?"

"Dmitri has told only a few close friends."

"Good." She pulled her shawl more closely around her and looked about the tiny room. "You know that after you left, the Committee for State Security froze all of our assets. Your mother and I managed as best we could with the money you sent. She did have to sell most of her jewelry."

Nikolai sighed.

Leading the way back to the front room, she unlocked a desk drawer and pulled out two envelopes. Handing Nikolai one, she said, "Here is the money we got from selling her emerald ring just before she died. Only the ruby necklace and earrings your father gave her when they became engaged are left."

Nikolai shook his head. "You keep it for all you've done."

"No, I did my duty for my sister. This belongs to you."

Nikolai took the envelope and put it in his pocket. "I am sorry, Aunt, that you had to go through all of this."

"Don't be. You did what you had to do."

Then she handed him the other envelope. "This letter is from your mother."

As Nikolai studied the envelope, his aunt went to the closet and removed a valise. “I am going to stay with my son. If you need me, call me there. Dmitri, can you drive me?”

“Of course. Let me take your bag.”

In the middle of the night, Beth awoke. Looking around her, at first, she wondered where she was. She got out of bed and slipped her robe on over her nightgown. Making her way down the broad, carpeted stairs, she saw a dim light coming from the kitchen. Nikolai sat at the table smoking a cigarette and holding a letter in his hand.

She entered the room and asked, “Is everything all right?”

“Memories—they are not always pleasant.” He gestured toward the letter.

Beth went to him. She stood behind him and put her hands on his shoulders.

“This must be difficult for you.”

“If my mother loved me, it would be worse. Even if she had just loved Amalia, I would have cared for her.”

“Amalia was your sister?”

“Yes,” he said, covering his brow with his hand.

Beth felt his body tremble beneath her touch and brought her face close to his ear. “I’m so sorry. What can I do?”

“Just stay near me,” he answered.

From behind him, she wrapped her arms around his shoulders and held him as she rested the side of her head against his.

When Beth awoke in the morning, she put on her robe and went downstairs. Nikolai sat at the table, dressed in clothes she had never seen before, smoking a cigarette.

He motioned to her to sit down. “Would you like coffee?”

When she nodded, he said, "Anna, kofye." Immediately, the woman brought her a steaming mug.

Beth sat down, bewildered. "Are you the same man that I left the United States with? Or do you have some twin brother who's playing a game of The Prince and the Pauper?"

"It is still me, Beth," he answered, looking over at her as he stubbed out the end of the cigarette in the ashtray.

"Well, I'm very confused. Whose house is this?"

"It belongs to a friend. He is letting us stay here."

"I thought the social classes didn't mix in Russia."

"He is simply repaying a debt he owes me. You must go and dress now for the funeral."

14

People from a funerary establishment delivered the coffin to the house and placed it on low pedestals in the parlor. Beth watched as they prepared for the viewing. They opened the top half of the coffin, and the woman lay against satin cushions, austere, and unsmiling even in death.

Only the closest friends and relatives came to the house to pay their respects. They all approached Nikolai and shook his hand to extend their condolences. As Beth stood by his side, trying to decipher as many words of sympathy as she possibly could, she was certain she heard one young man address Nikolai as "Professor."

Afterward, the casket was loaded into a black hearse, which proceeded toward the centuries-old stone cathedral with the funeral procession following. When Nikolai and Beth's car arrived, they followed the pallbearers up the steps through the massive Gothic doors.

An echoed hush pervaded the dimly lit interior. Dramatic elongated figures in Byzantine mosaic decorated the walls. Stone columns that lined the aisles soared to the vast heights of the arched Gothic ceiling. On the marble altar, gilded candelabras blazed surrounded by bouquets of white flowers.

As the mass began, ethereal music, which emanated from an ancient organ at the back of the church, filled the sanctuary. Beth sat close to Nikolai. Silently, she watched him, noticing that his countenance remained fixed and tearless, so unlike his emotional reaction to her mother's death just a few months ago.

Beth sensed that many of the eyes in the church were on her. Near the end of the long mass, the priest, dressed in white vestments, walked around the casket, shrouding it in the smoky mist of burning incense.

Then, the pallbearers carried the casket out into the brisk wind of the churchyard cemetery and placed it in a plot beside Nikolai's father. After the last prayers were said, people began to leave.

Nikolai walked to a nearby headstone and went down on one knee, bowing his head. Beth stood behind him. She could not read the Cyrillic alphabet, which comprised the letters on the stone, but she assumed this was the grave of his sister Amalia. Beth touched his shoulder, but he looked away from her.

They drove back to the big house where the funeral luncheon was to be served. As Nikolai and Beth entered the dining room, she looked around incredulously. Elaborate platters of food, which included exotically cooked fish and meats and many types of vegetables and salads, were arranged on the sideboard in the dining room. Another table boasted many fancy desserts.

Nikolai took her arm. "Shall we eat?"

"Everything looks wonderful, but who did all this?"

"Anna and her husband. They are very good at making Russian specialties. Now you must eat."

Beth got herself a plateful of food and set it on the table. Then she poured herself a cup of hot water for tea from what looked to be an elaborate but odd looking, large electric coffee pot with a spout. It seemed to be a modern version of the antique piece in the kitchen.

Nikolai walked over to her.

"What is this?" Beth asked.

"It is a samovar. Unlike the one in the kitchen, this one is electric," Nikolai answered.

"Such beautiful objects just to boil water for tea?"

He smiled. "Everyone thinks that the English are the only ones who love their tea, but the Russians have turned tea-drinking into an art."

"I never knew that," Beth said.

Beth sat down at one end of the dining room table with a few women. One of them was Nikolai's aunt, a stocky woman who appeared to be in her sixties. Her softly rounded features and light blue eyes gave her the healthy appearance of a farm matron.

She looked at Beth appraisingly as she conversed with a young woman, sitting beside her. This woman, a dark-eyed beauty with full languorous lips, also stared at Beth.

Beth could not understand much of what they said, but she knew they were talking about her. Occasionally, the young woman, named Marina, looked in her direction, and then she would glance over at Nikolai, who was sitting at the opposite end of the table with the men drinking vodka.

He had discarded his suit jacket and sat there in the white dress shirt that defined his broad chest and strong arms. He talked loudly in Russian, gesturing with his hands, thoroughly enjoying the conversation.

Beth had never seen him so animated. Although the vodka had something to do with this, she also knew the comfort he derived in being surrounded by his friends must play the largest role.

She suddenly felt fear. Would he want to come back to the United States now that he had seen what he was missing? And would the young woman, who kept staring at him and smiling seductively when she caught his glance, be a factor if he decided to stay?

Beth was tired to the bone, but she did not want to go to bed, leaving Nikolai at one end of the table and this woman at the other.

Dmitri downed a shot of vodka and said in halting English, "Nikolai, some friends will come to my house for my birthday tomorrow night. I hope you and Beth will come."

"Yes, we will be there," Nikolai answered good-naturedly as he raised his shot glass and looked at Beth.

Finally, the women rose to leave. They went over and kissed Nikolai good night. The young woman seemed to linger over the kiss and stared into Nikolai's eyes.

After they were gone, Beth made her way up to her room, and although she was tired, she could not sleep. For another hour the men drank and talked, but at last, they too departed. Beth heard Nikolai's unsteady step on the stairs. He paused for a moment at her door but then moved on down the hall to his own room.

Beth's jealousy over the dark-haired woman had somehow induced a flaming desire for him within her. She wished that in his drunken state, he had come into her room and begged her to make love. More than anything, she wanted to feel his hands upon her body.

A few hours later, still unable to sleep, she went down to the kitchen hoping to find him there, but as she suspected, the vodka must have lulled him into a deep sleep.

In the morning, when she walked into the kitchen, he was again giving the servants directives.

As she sat down with her coffee, he said, "We must hurry and get ready. I want to go and buy a birthday gift for Dmitri."

Beth shook her head, thinking of the days in the past when they sat in her kitchen, and she ordered him to hurry to get ready for class or begin his work for the day. Coming to Russia had not only involved traveling halfway around the world but had also caused the world as she knew it to be turned completely upside-down.

At eleven, they got into a small black car and started out for Nevsky Prospekt, the prime shopping district. They walked the busy thoroughfare with tall antique lampposts and myriad colorful buildings. Cathedrals, theaters, libraries, art studios, restaurants, and cafes lined the wide street, looking like a huge carnival or fair.

Nikolai held her by the elbow and warned, "Be careful of the gypsies. They send their children to distract you, and then the older ones steal your wallet. They can tell a foreigner right away."

Beth held her pocketbook under her arm as she tried to take in all the sights. High up on a billboard, she saw the familiar logo for Coca Cola and laughed. "I guess you can buy coke just about anywhere in the world."

"Believe me, it was a necessity to import it. We tried to manufacture our own, and it was a big disaster. They called it "Comrade Cola" and the taste was worse than the name."

Beth laughed.

They stopped at Gostiny Dvor, which consisted of columned arcades, forming entrances into individual kiosks.

"First, we must buy Dmitri a bottle of Shampanskoe," Nikolai said.

"What on Earth is that?" asked Beth.

"Russian wine. It tastes very much like champagne."

After they made their purchase, the couple walked along Nevsky Prospekt, and Nikolai filled her in on the history of the city.

"When Peter the Great captured this area from the Swedes, it was a large swamp. He drained the land and started building this beautiful city with its canals and bridges. Peter was so fascinated by European culture that he brought in Italian architects to build his city. He made it his "window on the west."

"Why was he so interested in European architecture?"

"Because Russia was not part of the Renaissance."

"Why not?"

"During that time of learning and advancement, we were ruled by the Mongols and so were influenced by the East. Once we threw off the Mongol yoke, we worked very hard to catch up to our neighbors in the west. That is one reason why we Russians were so proud to become a superpower and surpass all of the European nations."

Putting his hands in his pockets, Nikolai sighed. "And that is also why our recent fall to a lesser power was such a terrible disappointment. Still, many Russians have their place in history."

Beth and Nikolai passed the place where Nevsky Prospekt intersected Malaya Morskaya Ulitsa. He pointed at a house up the street. "Tchaikovsky lived there until he died."

"Really?" said Beth, intrigued by the idea that Tchaikovsky had walked the same streets that she now walked.

Nikolai looked at his watch and gestured at a nearby building. "Come, we will have lunch at my favorite restaurant."

Beth read the words Literaturnoye Kafé on a sign over the door. They went in and were seated at a round table. Dimly lit wall sconces cast dramatic shadows on the dark walls, and tall lamps set on wooden pedestals in the center of the room, illuminated the deep red tones of the floor.

Nikolai ordered wine for them. "Did you know that it was from this place that Pushkin left for his duel with D'Anthes?"

Beth felt delicious excitement as he retold the story of the duel. She was immersed in the sparkling intensity of his golden-green eyes that seemed to glow only for her. At least, she had always assumed these warm gazes were reserved only for her. But now she wondered if he also looked at other women in the same way—especially the young woman from the funeral dinner.

Jealousy with a barbed edge intruded into her thoughts. She wanted Nikolai, and she wanted him all to herself. She rationalized that there was no real evidence he was using her to become an American citizen. In all the time she had known him, he had treated her with only love and respect.

She watched him as he ordered lunch for both of them. He was a confident, even authoritative, man in his own country. Studying his dark handsome features, she ached to be held by him.

They finished their lunch and stopped for some groceries at Yeliseyev's. Nikolai looked over the items displayed on the shelves and under the counter in glass cases. Finally, he said, "Ah, yes, we need this."

"What is it?" asked Beth.

"Ikra, you know—caviar."

"I've never had it. Isn't it fish eggs?"

"Yes, from the sturgeon. It is very good for you. Nicholas II insisted that his children eat it on black bread with sliced bananas every morning."

"It doesn't sound too appetizing if you ask me."

"There are our other delicacies, too, like pony meat and shchuvak, which is camel's milk. Would you like to try them?"

"I'll pass this time," she said, laughing.

As Nikolai drove back to the house, he turned toward her and said, "You must wear something nice tonight. Russians dress up for birthday parties."

"Okay," she replied as she considered dresses she had brought.

15

Wondering if they would see Marina tonight, Beth took special care in getting ready for the party. She selected a black, fitted dress that came to the middle of her knee. It was sleeveless and was cut high on her creamy, white shoulders. The neckline was low enough to reveal the slope of her white breasts. Looking in the mirror, Beth checked her makeup and smoothed back a few wispy strands of hair.

When she descended the stairs, Nikolai seemed pleased. He looked handsome in black slacks and a black silk shirt with a gray sport jacket. As he helped her on with her coat, she could feel his hands through the garment, smoothing over her shoulders. Reveling in the warmth of his touch, she wanted to turn and place her palms on the sides of his face, guiding his lips to hers. But he picked up the car keys and led her to the door.

Dmitri's house was also lavish with antique furniture and crystal chandeliers. As Beth browsed, she saw the woman who had been at the funeral enter the front hall.

Marina handed her coat to the host and strode across the room to a group of women. Feeling out of place and a little jealous, Beth stayed close to Nikolai, but at times he would drift off to talk to an old friend.

It was at one of these times that Marina joined him. She took his hand and led him into the next room. They were gone for a few minutes when Beth decided that she must see what was going on, so she walked to the doorway.

Nikolai was leaning back against the wall with his hands in his pockets. The woman moved in closer, putting her hands on his chest and then moving them under his sport jacket around to his back. When he did not respond to her overtures, she looked up at him in a sultry, teasing manner.

Beth, angered by the woman's audacity, made a coughing noise and pretended to just be entering the doorway. Marina quickly backed away from Nikolai. She eyed Beth and walked out of the room. Beth glared at Nikolai and walked out too.

As she was getting herself a glass of wine, Marina approached her and spoke in English. "You do not mind that I touch Nikolai, do you? His aunt tells me that this marriage is in name only—that you and Nikolai do not sleep together."

Beth surveyed her coldly and said, "His aunt was mistaken."

Marina eyed Beth up and down again and then looked over at Nikolai. "You don't look like the kind of woman he desires."

"He'll have to speak for himself then." Beth trembled with rage as the woman slowly backed away from her.

Nikolai appeared to be amused as he drove back to the house. Beth said nothing to him. When they arrived home, she went directly up to her room. She could hear him coming up the stairs, but instead of going past her door, he opened it and walked in, shutting it behind him.

"What are you doing?" she asked.

He smiled. "There is something I must ask you."

She turned haughtily toward the mirror, taking off her earrings. "I'm sure anything you need to know Marina can tell you."

He came up behind her and placed a hand on her arm. "I have just heard something very pleasing."

Beth jerked her arm away. "Well, it can't be that Marina has the hots for you because you already knew that."

His smiled broadened. "It has to do with you."

Beth raised an eyebrow.

"Did you tell Marina that we are sleeping together?"

Beth went pale, remembering her lie.

"In a house where there are servants, information like this is known by them, and they are not good at keeping it to themselves. If we do not sleep together, you will look like a liar, and Marina will be very happy. Why did you tell her that?"

Beth leaned her palms on the bureau and shook her head. "I don't know. I just didn't like her hands all over you. I was protecting you from her pawing. You should thank me."

He came close behind her. "Maybe I want to be—how do you say—pawed."

Beth tried to move away from him, but he grabbed her arm and turned her toward him. "I want to be touched but not by Marina. I want to be touched by you."

"This is crazy. It's all ridiculous—even this marriage."

"It might not seem so ridiculous if you actually touched me. Here," he said as he grabbed her hands. "Touch my chest; it is not so bad." Then he moved her hands down to his stomach and to his thighs.

As he smoothed her hands over his thighs, she could feel the very tip of his erection through the pants, and she caught her breath.

"See, I like you. You make me crazy. You fight with me and call me names, but then you will not let another woman touch me. Come here, let me love you."

"Nikolai, we can't," she said, looking away from him.

"What is the harm? We are eight thousand miles from home in a beautiful house in the same bedroom. Come to me, Beth. Let me love you like a husband." He pulled her close and placed his hand on the side of her neck, caressing it with his thumb. Then he buried his face in her hair.

Her palms were still splayed against his chest, but the fight was out of her. She was dizzy with the scent of him, and what she wanted now was his hands on her body.

As her resistance disintegrated, Nikolai slipped his hand inside the low neckline of the dress and beneath the bra. She inhaled sharply when he caressed the nipple. He unbuttoned the top of the dress and slid the bra strap down, exposing her breast. She made no move to stop him. Nikolai pulled down the other strap. Cupping her breasts in his hands, he skimmed his lips over them, but when he came to the nipples, his lips parted, taking the warm taut flesh into his mouth.

In a state of agonizing ecstasy, she closed her eyes and moaned as she sensually offered one breast, then the other to him. He rapidly unfastened the rest of the buttons of the dress and pushed it off her shoulders, letting it fall at her feet. His hands were at her waist and then slid down beneath her silk panties, smoothing over her hips. Her arms came around his neck, and yielding, she pressed her body against him.

He whispered in her ear, "Beth, do you love me?"

"Yes," she answered as he caressed her body intimately.

"Even though I am a just a carpenter?"

"Yes," she insisted more urgently

"But I am a peasant."

"I don't care. I love you," she said desperately as she moved her hands on his back.

He picked her up and laid her on the bed. Pulling the combs from her long hair, he knelt over her, kissing her shoulder, the hollow place between her breasts, and then her belly.

Every place his mouth touched burned with an explosive fire, and she held her breath, praying he wouldn't stop. Then Beth took his calloused hands in hers and kissed them—the palms, the fingertips. Now, she understood these hands had dignity because of the work they did.

He quickly engulfed her in his arms and sounding almost as if he were choking with tears, he pressed his face into her neck and said, "This must be forever, Beth. You can never again keep me from your bed."

"It will be forever, my love," she answered breathlessly.

Letting go of all of her doubts, Beth passionately surrendered her body to him. He knelt above her touching her breasts as he looked into her eyes intently, almost as if he would never see her again. She reveled in each touch, his hands moving intimately over her body, her moans revealing the ecstatic pleasure of his lovemaking.

His steamy kisses left her trembling with desire, and in her desperate need for him, her lips met his with scalding intensity. She tilted her head back, and shivers of desire swept through her as she felt his lips and the roughness of his cheek on her neck, and she took in the sweet, masculine scent of his hair. His mouth found her warm, supple breasts, and cupping them in his palms, he kissed them with a tortured groan. Then taking each dark areola deeply into his mouth, he flicked his tongue across each one with staccato-like movements that made her catch her breath.

In their fiery obsession for one another, he grasped her close, and their bodies arched together urgently as he entered her. Moving together in the wildest of passions, they reached an exquisitely erotic climax, and they clung together oblivious to the world around them. As he whispered tender words of love, his hands moved slowly over her body, and she shivered in the afterglow of their lovemaking.

Later, they slept with their naked bodies pressed together. With her face against the back of his neck, her soft long hair brushed across her cheek and cascaded over his shoulder. Her knee was slung over his hip, and his hand rested possessively on top of it.

During the night, he woke her and pushing her hair back off her face, made love to her again. Beth held nothing back from him. She was his—body and soul.

The next morning when she awoke, she reached for him, remembering their night of lovemaking, but he was not there. Before she could get out of bed, he entered the room, fully clothed. Coming over to her with a look of satisfaction on his face, he pulled down the sheet and leaned on the bed on one knee. Holding her hands at her sides against the sheets, he playfully nipped at her shoulder with his teeth. Then he gently bit her breast and nipped at her hip. She laughed, and freeing her arms, she wrapped them around his neck, pulling his head down to hers. Looking into her eyes, he said, "You must get up. We are going sightseeing today."

"Do we have to?"

"Yes, there are some important places you must see," he answered, cocking his head off to the side as she had seen him do so many times before.

"How important can they be?" she asked, pulling him down onto the bed with her.

He grinned. "I see that you have not had enough of me yet." Unbuckling his belt, he said, "I will have to remedy this situation."

She smiled back at him as she unbuttoned his shirt.

When they were at last in the car heading for the center of the city, he pulled her close to him and drove with his arm around her. She pressed her head against his shoulder, thinking she had not done this since she was in high school.

They drove down Nevsky Prospekt, and at the end of it, they turned down a side street and parked the car. Along the lovely tree-lined streets, he pointed out St. Isaac's Cathedral with bright sunshine glinting off its golden dome and the Admiralty building with its rows of columns and towering spire. Walking farther, they stopped to lean on the ornate wrought iron railing that lined the sparkling Neva River and looked toward Vasilyievsky Island. From their vantage point, Nikolai pointed out St. Petersburg University.

Beth said, "What a magnificent city. Is the rest of Russia this beautiful?"

"There are many beautiful places, but there are many places that are contaminated. Unfortunately, Chernobyl is not the worst nuclear accident we have had."

"Really?"

"Yes, I have read in a study that by 2020 most Russian babies will be born with health problems."

"That's awful. I wouldn't want to be raising a child here."

"Russian mothers have no choice."

"Nikolai, where did you read that study?"

He shrugged. "At St. Petersburg University."

"I knew it! You were a student there, weren't you?"

"Yes," he replied as he leaned his elbows on the wrought iron railing and stared at the university across the river. "But, I was not only a student. I was also a professor there."

She let out an exasperated sound. "You scoundrel!"

Smiling at her feigned anger, he pulled her close and asked, "What is a scoundrel?"

"A person who takes advantage of another person's innocence. Why did you go through this whole charade of pretending to be a peasant and a carpenter?"

"Because I wanted you to love me for myself, not for my position."

"Well, it seems a little extreme to me, but I certainly learned that lesson well. Damn, and I just got used to you as a carpenter."

"This time when we go back to the U.S., I will look into getting a position in the science department at Fairfield University. There will be no more late night rides, trying to get false licenses and social security numbers."

"Is that what you were doing? I was worried that you were out with girls."

"So, you cared for me even then?"

"Longer than you know, so much longer, but I needed to know about you and your life."

"I was a professor of astrophysics. The government tried to force me to work for them on a secret weapons program. But I was unwilling because I want to use my knowledge to help people, not hurt them. However, in Russia the powers that rule do not take 'no' for an answer. So I had to flee the country, and in doing this, left my mother at the mercy of those who wanted to hurt me."

"What did they do to her?" asked Beth.

"First they stopped my father's pension that went to her each month. Then they controlled all her assets, so that she could not have access to them. That was why she depended on me to send money."

"But, why didn't you ask for political asylum once you got to the U.S.? I'm sure the government would have granted it, considering your field of expertise."

He sighed. "My government and yours are working on a secret project and one provision of it is that Russian defectors must be sent back to Russia."

"That's terrible. What could be so important that the American government would send back people who are seeking asylum?"

"Many small countries that used to belong to the Soviet Union possess dangerous nuclear material. Both governments are cooperating to get all of it and store it in a safe place."

"Still, it doesn't seem right."

He nodded. "Yes, but they do it for the good of many not the few."

Beth chewed her lip. "So, you went through all that hardship and humiliation because of your principles?"

"Yes."

"Did anyone know the truth?"

"Yes," he said, staring across the river. "Your mother."

"But, Nikolai, why would you tell her and not me?"

"I didn't tell you because it would put you in a difficult position."

"Did you think I would turn you in?"

"No, but you might have let me go, and I couldn't allow that to happen."

"Were you worried about getting another job?"

He turned toward her. "Beth, I was in love with you from the first time I saw you, and I desperately wanted to be near you. Also, I was determined to make you love me even if you thought I was just a carpenter."

She took his hand and said, "Carpenter or physicist, I have never loved anyone the way I love you."

He brought her hand to his lips. "For this I am glad because you are the true love of my life."

"What about Olga or Marina?" she teased.

"I want only you," he said, pulling her close to him.

With his arm around her, they strolled along the Neva River toward the Winter Palace. The sunlit water reflected a shimmering parade of ornate pastel-colored buildings.

As they walked, Beth saw a car with a teddy bear tied to the front grill.

"Why on earth would someone tie a teddy bear onto their car?" she asked.

"Look inside the car. What do you see?"

"A bride and groom."

"Yes, and the teddy bear means they want their first child to be a boy. If they want a girl, they use a doll."

"Does the system work?" she laughed.

"I don't know. Maybe we should try it and see." He hugged her to him with one arm and nuzzled her ear. "We could, you know. We are married." He pulled her around, pinning her against the wrought iron railing. Putting his hands inside her long coat and pulling her close, he buried his face in her hair. He moved his hands to her belly, smoothing his palms over the soft flatness of it and said, "I want you to have my baby. I want to feel my child moving within you."

Beth held his face in her hands and kissed his temple, his cold cheek, and then brushed his lips with hers. She whispered, "Yes, we will have a baby. I want that, too."

For the first time in her life, Beth wanted a child and did not view the idea of pregnancy as an interruption in her career but as a beautiful serious choice that would change her forever.

With his arm around her, they continued to the Palace Square.

"Since we must leave for the U.S. soon, I want to show you the most important places in the city."

"I almost wish we could stay. We're so happy here. If it weren't for my job at the university, we could. Even Immigration wouldn't care since we never gave them a definite day of our return."

"Russia is not a good place to live since the Fall. It is now a disorganized country, ruled by corrupt officials, unscrupulous business men, and the Mafiya."

"It's such a shame this beautiful country has so many problems," she said.

Nikolai smiled a cavalier grin. "Don't feel too sorry. There is a well-known proverb that says, 'Russia is always defeated but never beaten.'"

Making their way around a huge block of attached buildings, Nikolai and Beth entered the pastel-colored Winter Palace.

The sheer size of the rooms and the heavily ornate baroque décor was overwhelming. Pure white walls and vast gold-trimmed Palladian windows lined the walls. Above them ran a fancy balustrade in front of clerestory windows.

Beth stood in the middle of the room and turned around to take it all in. Marble stairways and statues adorned the rooms and immense crystal chandeliers hung from the ceilings.

She gasped in delight. "Oh, it's so lovely!"

"This is just one of the many palaces to be found in the city. Within this one is the museum called the Hermitage. Did you know it has three million pieces of art?"

"That's unbelievable."

"It is true. Most were purchased by Catherine the Great. It is said if you spent one minute looking at each picture, it would take you eighteen years to see the entire collection."

Beth laughed and took his arm. "Well, I guess we should get started.

16

By late afternoon, they were in the car returning home. Sitting close to him, Beth asked, "Nikolai, who owns the house we're staying in?"

He looked across at her. "I do, now. It was our family home, but since my parents and my sister are dead, it is mine."

Then somewhat hesitantly Beth continued, "Will you keep the house?"

"Yes, I will keep it."

"Why? Are you planning to come back here to live?"

Gently cupping her cheek in his palm, he said, "Do you think I could ever leave you? My home is where you are."

Beth exhaled a breath of relief. "Then what will you do with it?"

"I will close it up. Dmitri will oversee it for me. Do not worry," he answered, running his free hand along her thigh.

In the kitchen, Nikolai asked, "Would you like a cup of tea?"

"I'd love one," she answered, feeling deliriously happy with her husband and her life.

As he heated the water, he said, "This tea is special. It is served with a little rum in it."

"Are you trying to get me drunk?"

"Yes, then I will take advantage of you." He pulled her to him.

Beth wrapped her arms around his neck and let him kiss her deeply. His tongue sought hers. The open kiss became more sensual, and she moaned as he moved his hands on her back.

At that moment, the door opened and Anna, the maid, came in. Quickly, she excused herself and left the room.

With his mouth hovering above Beth's, Nikolai laughed. "She is Marina's aunt. It will not be long before news of us kissing in the kitchen will be passed on."

"Good," said Beth. "I want her to know you belong to me."

"Yes, but she must report more than a kiss. We will finish this upstairs."

Taking his hand, she led the way to her room, and he began to slowly undress her. Although his hands were calloused, they moved on her skin with cat-like softness that sent shivers up her spine. With her blouse pushed back off her shoulders and her bra straps hanging loosely around her upper arms, his warm mouth brushed her lips, her collarbone, and then found her exposed breasts. Quickly, Nikolai and Beth discarded their clothes and moved into each other's arms, writhing in exquisite splendor on the satin sheets.

After their lovemaking, with Nikolai's head resting in her arms, Beth remembered the words of Pushkin poetry:

> . . . By his swift, trembling hands,
> By the heat of his breath,
> By the soft and burning mouth
> Do you know your lover . . .

Beth and Nikolai lay in each other's arms. She awoke to his butterfly kisses on her eyelids and smiled up at him.

"We must get up. Today, we are going sightseeing again."

"Where?"

"Sennaya Ploshchad. You will like it. There are many things to do."

After their coffee, they drove out of the tree-lined driveway toward their destination.

In Sennaya Ploshchad, they parked on a side street and headed for the colorful, bustling marketplace. They browsed the many kiosks dappled in sunlight and haggled with the local vendors.

They stopped for lunch in a cheerful café with tiled walls and floral patterned curtains. After Nikolai ordered wine for both of them, he smiled across the table at her and said, "I have a surprise for you."

"What is it?"

"Tonight, we are going to the ballet to see *Swan Lake*."

"But, I've already seen it."

"Not with Russian ballet dancers. First, we must buy you a proper evening dress."

After the lunch of cold, marinated chicken, Nikolai and Beth perused the nearby stores. In a chic shop, they bought an elegant black dress with spaghetti straps. The front of the dress was low cut and showed the white creamy swell of her breasts. The waist was fitted, but the skirt flared.

That evening in the provocative black dress, Beth put her hair up and added color to her lips and cheeks.

Nikolai was waiting for her at the bottom of the stairs

When she reached him, he looked down at her and put his hand on the side of her neck, massaging the hollow of her cheek with his thumb. "I think being in Russia has done you some good because you look more beautiful than ever, and you look happier."

She put her hand over his. "I am happier because now I am truly your wife."

"Yes, and because you are truly my wife, I have something for you. He went to the massive hutch and opened one of the glass-paned, doors. From within it, he extracted a velvet box. "Come here," he said.

She came close, and when he opened the top, she caught her breath. A gold necklace with a large, square, ruby pendant and earrings to match shone against the dark velvet lining of the box. It was obvious that the jewels were antique because the gems were cut so that the facets came to a point at the center of the stone, and the gold settings were lacy filigree.

Nikolai turned her toward a large gilded mirror and standing behind her, he fastened the necklace with the sure hands of a husband.

"My father gave these jewels to my mother when they became engaged. I am giving them to you as a wedding present."

Looking in the mirror, Beth admired the necklace as she carefully put the earrings on. Then, she turned toward him with misty eyes and said, "Oh, Nikolai, how beautiful they are."

Nikolai touched the gleaming pendant where it lay just above her collarbone and said, "The gems pale against your beauty."

After parking the car, they walked the quiet street along the canal toward the Mariinsky Theater.

Nikolai stopped and looked up at the night sky. He took a deep breath of the cold evening air and put an arm around her shoulder. "The stars, they are jewels in the sky—hundreds of millions of them between us and the cosmic horizon. And tonight my joy reaches that high."

Enthralled by the beautiful words, Beth placed her hand on his chest. “You will always be the most beautiful part of my life.”

“And you will be mine.” He moved his head down to hers and kissed her.

Inside the theatre, Beth was overwhelmed by its sumptuousness. Gilded ornate trim and cameo medallions adorned the walls, and imperial eagles decorated the royal box. Even the ceilings were painted with dancing girls and cupids.

As they took their seats in the semi-dark theater, Nikolai whispered, “I saw Nureyev perform the lead in *Swan Lake* here before he defected years ago.”

As total darkness engulfed the theater, the curtain, consisting of a multitude of veiled layers, went up, revealing glittering palace scenery and the entourage of lavish costumes. Ballerinas, dressed in pastel tulle, balanced on tiptoes while men in white tights twirled around them as they performed the love story of Prince Siegfried and the swan maiden, Odette. The graceful beauty of the dancers and the intense drama of each scene brought tears to Beth’s eyes.

Nikolai sat close to her and occasionally moved his head near to whisper something to her. Sitting in this magnificent theater with her handsome husband, Beth couldn’t help but compare it to the dull evening she had spent with Brad Wilson.

In the car afterward, Nikolai said, “We will go to Dmitri’s for a little while.”

Beth searched her purse for lipstick. “We better not stay too late because we have the flight home tomorrow.”

“We will not stay long,” Nikolai answered.

The gathering of people at Dmitri's was the same as those who had attended the funeral. Among them was Marina.

As Beth and Nikolai walked into the house, Beth reveled in Nikolai's embrace. With one arm wrapped around her, he looked down at her, beaming with love.

Glancing around the room, Beth saw Marina at the far end with her arms folded across her chest, glaring at her. However, when the woman focused on the ruby earrings and necklace, a vitriolic hatred blazed in her eyes.

Dmitri poured shots of vodka as the happy couple joined the group.

"Now, you must drink," he insisted, looking at Nikolai and Beth.

Beth laughed. "I can't. I've never drunk vodka straight."

"You can do it, Beth," said Nikolai. "But, first you must take in a deep breath and that will lessen the fiery taste."

They both followed the procedure Nikolai suggested and downed the shots. When Nikolai handed her another, again she drank with him. He laughed and took her in his arms, rocking her back and forth and nuzzling his face in her hair.

As the evening progressed, Nikolai became engrossed in conversation with the men. Beth went into the bathroom to check her make-up. When she came out, Marina was standing by the door. Beth thought the woman wanted to go in, so she walked past her, excusing herself. But, Marina followed her to a small group of women.

With one hand on her hip she looked at Beth and sneered, "So, you have married Nikolai to give him citizenship in the United States, and you think he loves you."

She repeated this in Russian to the other women standing around her. They giggled knowingly. Finally, one of them said in a heavy Russian accent, "Never, never believe that a man loves you if he wants citizenship. He will tell any lie to get it. He may say he loves you, but you can never know the truth."

Marina laughed. "I have seen many women tricked into believing this kind of foolishness, but they are always alone in the end." When she translated this into her own language, again, they all knowingly agreed.

Beth listened to what they said, trying to convince herself this couldn't be true in her case, but those women who spoke English kept bringing up example after example of Russian men marrying American women and then divorcing them after five years.

Beth felt numb. Her mind reeled as she tried to distance the stories she heard from her own experience. She thought of Nikolai and his passionate lovemaking. Last night he had awakened her in the middle of the night, hungry for her even though they had had sex only a few hours before. Would a man go through all that to try to fool a woman concerning his love?

Beth remembered the intensity of his lovemaking and his vows to love her forever. "But couldn't all of this be faked?" she wondered. Then she recalled her own passion. She certainly did not have to fake the orgasms she had had when he made love to her.

With doubt invading her thoughts, Beth remembered the unbridled passion she had revealed to him and wondered if he possibly could have been toying with her. Suddenly, her face flushed, and she felt like a fool. Keeping control of herself, she walked away and stood near Nikolai, waiting to go home.

On the drive home, she didn't speak.

Nikolai looked over at her. "Beth, are you all right?"

"Yes," she answered, but stared straight ahead.

When they reached the house, she went directly up to her room.

Nikolai followed her up the stairs. Once in the room, he asked, "Beth, what is it?"

Refusing to answer him, she walked to the bureau and removed the earrings and necklace.

He went to her and put his hands on her shoulders. "Please tell me what is wrong."

She twisted out of his grasp. "Don't touch me."

"What has happened?" he asked, his voice rising.

"Those women tonight, they filled me in on a little Russian history that you conveniently forgot to tell me. I heard about all the Russian men who duped unsuspecting American women into marrying them so they could become citizens."

"Do you not know that Marina is jealous of you? She will say anything to keep us apart."

"Well, she wasn't the only one telling the stories. The other women knew men who had done the same thing. They said these men act as if they are crazy about the women until the five years are up. Then, they drop them and never look back."

Beth felt her eyes mist. Turning away from him, she leaned her palms on the dresser. The mirror reflected the tears that streamed down her cheeks and her breasts straining against the silk bodice of the dress.

Nikolai came up behind her and seized her shoulders. "We have been through this citizenship problem before. Why are you suddenly obsessed with it again?"

"Because everything I worried about then seems to be truer than I thought."

Lowering her head, Beth cried softly. She could feel his hands on her shoulders and his breath on her neck as he pleaded, "You know my love is true."

"How can I believe you? I hate you! You've made a fool out of me," she screamed.

In her hysterics, she felt the spaghetti straps of the dress fall around her upper arms, and with each sob, her breasts heaved against the thin material of the low-cut bodice.

Nikolai put his hands on her waist, but Beth strained against his grasp and hissed, "Don't touch me!"

He moved in close behind her, and over her protests, held her tightly against him. Pressing his face against the side of her neck, he begged, "Beth, you know I am crazy for you! I can't live without you. Please, please, Beth, do not do this."

She stopped resisting him for a moment and hung her head, letting her tears fall. Quickly his hands covered her breasts, and he pressed his mouth to her ear. “Beth, please . . . please listen to me.”

She grabbed his hands, trying to remove them, but in the heat of the moment, she pressed them more deeply into the warm flesh. His lips scalded her neck. She turned her head toward him. His mouth hungrily found hers, and for an instant, their lips met in a searing kiss.

Mustering all of her strength, she wrenched herself free and whirled around to face him. “It’s over, Nikolai. Please, leave me alone.”

He pleaded, “Beth, listen to me. The only real moment we have in this life is the blessed now. Let us live for this moment.”

He placed his hands high on the sides of her waist. “We must talk about this when we are not so excited. Let me soothe you. Come with me to the bed. I will lie down with you and calm you.”

“I can’t allow myself to be used,” she cried, beating her fists on his chest.

“Listen to me, my love. You know you are not being used. I love you desperately.”

She pushed him away. “Every time we made love, I would wonder.”

Nikolai pulled her against him. She could feel his breath on her neck and shoulder. His mouth hovered just above hers. “I cannot let you go. I have loved you since the day I met you.”

She lowered her head. “Please don’t make this any harder on either of us. It’s over.”

He lifted her chin, and she met his gaze. “Your pride will be the end of both of us.” With tears in his eyes, he moved away from her and walked out the door.

Beth flung herself on the bed and sobbed.

Nikolai sat in a chair in his room the whole night as tears streamed down his face. Words written by the hapless poet Pushkin came back to him:

"Love gives one instant of unspeakable joy
And the misery that follows lasts until death."

In the morning, acting very business-like, Beth brought her luggage into the foyer.

Nikolai leaned in the open doorway smoking a cigarette and watching the smoke drift away in the mild Russian breeze. It was obvious that she had not changed her mind. He threw his cigarette in the grass and walked outside.

Dmitri waited, standing beside his car. He and Nikolai loaded the suitcases into the trunk. Beth came out and stood for a long moment staring at the house. Then she got into the car.

That morning she had left the ruby pendant and earrings on the hall table. She noticed on the way out they were no longer there. Also, Beth was sure that Marina had already received the news that she and Nikolai were no longer sleeping in the same bed.

17

The Aeroflot plane back to the U.S. was overcrowded and uncomfortable. Nikolai and Beth sat side by side in the compact seats for the long flight. But no matter the conditions, Nikolai realized Beth's anger was so great she would not even allow her arm or shoulder to touch his.

When they reached home, he silently helped her carry her luggage into the house. Both emotionally and physically exhausted, he went into his room and fell asleep.

Nikolai waited for Beth to come out of her room on Sunday. But with no sign of her by the middle of the afternoon, he went outside to do some raking. He kept thinking of Beth and wondered how they could ever be together again. Being so near to her but unable to touch her only heightened his burning desire for her.

In the morning, Nikolai entered the kitchen and poured himself a cup of coffee. He sat opposite Beth. Wisps of her soft hair escaped the pins that held it up and brushed against her white neck as she read the newspaper. When she folded the paper, he cleared his throat and asked, "Can you give me a ride to the university? I want to see if there is a possibility of a job for me."

Beth nodded as she got up and put her cup in the sink.

The drive to school was a silent one, and when it ended, each of them got out of the car and went in different directions—Beth to her first class and Nikolai to the Dean of Faculty. Dean Avery, a robust, balding man in his fifties, was very impressed with Nikolai's credentials.

Taking off his horned-rimmed glasses, he leaned back in his leather chair to discuss a preliminary position of adjunct professor with advancement to full professor as soon as it could be arranged. For now, Nikolai would give guest lectures for the science department.

A few mornings later, Nikolai came into the kitchen. Beth was sitting at the table, drinking coffee. Her cheeks and lush lips were colored with the blush of sleep, and the curves of her beautiful body showed beneath the satin robe which was tied at the waist.

Trying to control his intense desire for her, Nikolai turned away from her to pour himself a cup of coffee. "Beth, I have been to the university and talked to Dean Avery. He has offered me a position in the Science Department, starting immediately."

She said, "That's surprising since it's so late in the semester."

"He thinks I will be an asset to the department because I can teach more advanced classes. Also, I asked him for housing on campus."

He turned toward her and met her gaze. "I cannot live here and never touch you again"

She looked down. "What about immigration? I thought we were supposed to make them believe we were living together as husband and wife?"

Nikolai shrugged. "They have not been here since we came back. I will leave some of my clothes in the closet and personal things in the bathroom. That might be enough to keep them happy."

"What if it's not?" asked Beth.

"Then, I will come to you and see what can be done."

"Okay," replied Beth with uncertainty in her voice. "Will you come for your mail?"

Nikolai thought about coming back to this house daily or weekly for his mail and knew it would be difficult for both of them. He shook his head. "No, I will have my mail sent to the school."

He opened the back door and went outside. Removing the pack of Camels from his shirt pocket, he tapped one out. As he took the first drag, he looked toward the house. Beth was watching through the window. When their eyes met, she turned away. He remembered his promise to her mother to take care of Beth, but he knew he could not stay with her this way.

The university quickly provided Nikolai with a small apartment on campus, and by the end of the week, most of his things had been removed from Beth's house. Before he left, he stood for a long while staring at Mrs. Winters' perennial garden, which now was a mass of bright red tulips and yellow daffodils.

Nikolai wiped tears from his eyes with the back of his hand as he remembered the older woman and all the kindness she had shown him.

When he turned toward the house, he saw Beth watching him through the window—her own tears streaking down her face.

When Nikolai's cousin arrived to take him to his apartment, Beth came down and met him in the foyer where the last of his things were piled. In one box were the radio and CDs she and her mother had bought him for Christmas. In another, were the leather bound books she had bought for him. Again, her eyes filled with tears.

Nikolai came close but didn't touch her. "I am going now, but you know that my heart remains here with you."

Beth looked into his eyes, but the intensity in them made her look away.

She spoke softly, "If there's a problem with immigration, please let me know. I don't want something to happen to you on my account."

"There will not be a problem." He stared at her for a long moment. Then he picked up the boxes and walked out of the house. He got into his cousin's car and sped away.

Beth crumpled on the front step and wept.

Nikolai gradually became accustomed to his new surroundings and enjoyed lecturing, but his mind was always on Beth—her face, her body, her smile. All came back to him with a blinding clarity that pierced his heart. He wanted her more than he wanted anything in his life, and the fact that he couldn't have her filled him with excruciating pain. Again, the words of the poet, Pushkin came to mind:

> "What I would give . . . one dark night,
> To sweep you up in my arms,
> Gaze upon you with languorous eyes . . .
> Listen in ecstasy and delight
> To your fervent murmur, your weary pleas . . ."

For Beth, the house felt like a tomb now that Nikolai was gone. The day after he left, she opened the closet and touched the collars of his shirts. When she came to his wedding suit, she pulled it out and hugged it to her, murmuring his name over and over.

Often she turned on the country music radio station because she missed the sound of it. Lying across Nikolai's bed, she would read and reread the melancholy love poems of Pushkin. Steeped in the mysterious dark beauty of Russia, they reminded her of Nikolai.

Because Nikolai's lectures were of a scientific nature, he and Beth never taught classes in the same building. But they did see each other walking on campus. Although they did not speak, their lingering glances told volumes.

Nikolai wanted to talk to Beth but every time he saw her, she always walked away quickly. One night as he listened to his country music CDs, Nikolai realized that the singers were expressing the same emotions that he was feeling. Suddenly, he thought of a way to communicate with Beth.

One afternoon as Beth approached her car, she saw a small piece of folded paper stuck under her windshield wiper. Removing it, she looked at the message and recognized the words as lines from a country song, written in Nikolai's handwriting. The note read:

> "When twilight falls, and the stars draw near,
> who will be there for all the years
> to comfort you and calm your fears,
> only me, your own true love."

She leaned against the side of the car and cried silently.

At home that evening, Beth sat at the kitchen table, staring at Nikolai's note when she heard a knock at the back door.

In her casual way, Doreen Johnson pushed it open and stepped inside. "Hey, what's up?"

Pulling out a chair opposite Beth, she sat with her hands folded on the table and searched Beth's face. "What's wrong?"

Beth tapped the side of Nikolai's note on the table and exhaled deeply. "Doreen, this is something you can't tell anyone. That's why I didn't call you right away."

"For God's sake, Beth, you know I'll keep your secret."

Beth exhaled. "Nikolai and I are separated."

"What happened?"

Beth shook her head. "You know the whole wedding thing occurred so he could go back to Russia and return without a problem. But something happened in Russia, and suddenly I really wanted to be married to him."

"That seems like a good thing."

"Yeah, but then I talked to this woman who gave me a little background on Russian men."

"What did she say?"

"Well basically that all Russian men who marry American women are divorced in five years."

"Do you think that's true?"

Beth ran a hand through her hair. "I know he cares for me, but I can't be sure he doesn't have an ulterior motive."

Doreen chewed on her lip. "He just didn't seem like that kind of guy."

"I know, and to make matters worse, I miss him terribly."

"Where is he?"

Beth propped her elbow on the table and rested her forehead in her palm. "He got an apartment at the university."

"Will he be all right . . . with immigration, I mean."

"I told him to call me if there was a problem."

"What are you going to do now?"
Shaking her head, she said, "I really don't know."

Two days later when Beth entered the cafeteria to meet some colleagues, she saw Nikolai sitting at a table across the room with professors from the Science Department. He had been talking animatedly when she entered, but the minute he saw her, he stopped speaking and stared in her direction. They sat at opposite ends of the room, transfixed by the electrically charged atmosphere but were unable to move toward each other.

After a while, Nikolai's friends rose to leave, and he walked out with them, taking a long last look at her before he disappeared through the door. Beth tried to seem cheerful in front of her colleagues, but her heart sank as he left.

Later, in the parking lot, Beth found another note with country lyrics beneath the windshield wiper of her car. This one read:

> "The pain of two lonely hearts can be found
> when a man and a woman are standing too proud.
> Their love burns away in a tirade of angry words
> that leaves them brokenhearted and lonely in an uncaring world."

Beth looked around hoping to see him somewhere nearby, but he was gone. She pressed the note against her heart as she got into her car. Tearfully, she considered his message on the way home. Beth remembered her mother's affection for Nikolai and his kind way of helping her remain positive until the end of her life. Beth thought about Nikolai's wild theories of other dimensions in space where souls could rest and wondered if her mother was in such a place. She also wondered what her mother might think of this terrible separation.

18

One month after Nikolai had moved out of Beth's house, immigration officials showed up at Dean Avery's office. They presented their case against Nikolai and insisted that the dean call him in for a meeting. The shaken administrator not only called Nikolai to his office but also called the university's lawyer, Bob Loftus.

As Nikolai walked toward the dean's office, he wondered if a new position had opened up for him. However, when he entered the room and saw the men, he knew the game was up.

In the dean's office, Attorney Loftus sat in a chair and bent his thin frame over his leather briefcase on the floor next to him. He pulled out a legal pad and pen and sat back. He smiled, creating elongated dimples in his gaunt face. Straightening his metal-rimmed glasses, he glanced at his watch. "So, what's the problem?"

Agent Robbins, a man of medium build with sandy hair and clear blue eyes, leaned forward in his seat and clasped his hands in front of him. He looked at Attorney Loftus as he spoke, "Mr. Mendeleyev was a well-known scientist in Russia. He was ordered to leave his teaching post at St. Petersburg University and begin work on a certain weapons project for his government. Because he refused, his punishment was to do hard labor at a Siberian prison camp. Somehow, he escaped the country and made his way here—illegally, I might add. A couple of months ago, he married a woman named Beth Winters. Now it appears that the couple is estranged, so to make a long story short, he has no legal right to stay in this country. He has to be deported as an illegal alien."

Attorney Loftus leaned forward and peered through his glasses at Nikolai. "Is all of this true?"

Nikolai looked down at his hands. "Yes, it is true."

Attorney Loftus removed his glasses and holding them in one hand, gestured toward Nikolai. "You are still legally married to this woman?"

Nikolai bit his lip. "Yes, we are still married, but we are not living together at this moment."

"May I ask why?" the lawyer queried.

"Right now, there are things we do not agree on."

Attorney Loftus put his glasses back on. "Well then, why don't we get in touch with her and see if we can't iron out some of these issues?"

The lawyer turned toward the officials and smiled. "Certainly, you boys can't object to that?"

Before either of them could speak, Nikolai said, "I will not call her."

The attorney spun around toward Nikolai. "Come now, there are very few disagreements that can't be settled when they are looked at objectively."

"No, I will not call her," Nikolai said, staring at the floor.

The lawyer cleared his throat. "Mr. Mendeleyev, if you don't call your wife, there is a very good chance you will be deported. Why not try to work something out?"

"No," Nikolai answered, lowering his head. He would not go to her for help because he knew this would only reinforce her belief that he was using her for citizenship and that he really did not love her. He would be deported and die in a Russian prison camp before he would let her think that. His life was over anyway. Without her, he did not want to live.

The lawyer looked at the immigration officials. "What if he applies for political asylum? He's a prime candidate for that."

The other man said, "In the present political environment, that is not possible. However, because he is such a high-profile scientist, we may secretly give him asylum under certain conditions."

"Okay, what does that entail?"

"If he is willing to work for the U.S. on certain weapons projects, we will provide asylum. If not, he goes back."

The lawyer looked at Nikolai and smiled. "What do you say? It sounds like a good deal to me."

"No," replied Nikolai evenly.

"Why?" gasped the lawyer.

"Because it is against my principles."

"For God's sake, Nikolai, you might as well do it and save yourself. If you don't, someone else will."

"No," he answered, staring at the opposite wall.

"Then, I can't help you." The lawyer dropped his hands lifelessly and shook his head.

"I will go back," said Nikolai without emotion.

Dean Avery pleaded with the men from immigration. "Listen, if you make him go back to Russia, he'll be arrested."

"Our hands are tied," said Agent Robbins, standing with feet apart in military position.

"There must be something else we can do. He's a noted physicist for God's sake," the lawyer said. "There's got to be a way around this. Can you give him some time to think about it?"

"We were instructed to bring him in. It's his decision."

Nikolai continued to stare at the opposite wall.

"Okay, let's go," said the other official, a heavyset man with dark hair and piercing black eyes, as he pulled Nikolai to his feet and hustled him toward the door.

In the car, the heavyset man drove as he talked on the phone. Agent Robbins sat in the back with Nikolai.

The man in front snapped his phone shut. He glanced over at Nikolai. "Let's see how you like dealing with the CIA."

Back at Nikolai's apartment, the government men told him to pack some things quickly. He filled two large duffle bags. When he had finished, he tore a piece of paper from a pad and scribbled a note.

Agent Robbins snatched the paper away from him and read it. "What's this?" he asked.

Nikolai said, "A last note for my wife."

The three of them walked through the parking lot. As they neared Beth's car, Nikolai stuck the note under her windshield wiper. He stood there watching it flutter in the breeze for a long moment before the men grabbed his arm and pushed him toward their black sedan.

Beth left the building where her last class was held and walked out into the late April sunshine. As she loaded her books into the car, she noticed another note under her windshield wiper. Retrieving it, she sat in the car, reading the words from a country song that Nikolai had put down on paper:

> "Although a long life may not be mine,
> my love for you will never die.
> And the passion that blazed between the two of us
> cannot end with the passing of one."

The tone of this note sent a chill of panic up Beth's spine. The words had a sense of foreboding about them. She hoped that immigration officials had not discovered their separation. Thoughts of Nikolai spending the rest of his life in a Siberian prison camp made her shudder. She consoled herself, remembering he'd promised to come to her if he had a problem with these people.

At home, she sat in her room and opened the hand-painted trinket box he had given her for Christmas. She picked up the white feather and closed her eyes as she brushed it against her lips. Looking at the picture on the box, she remembered the lovers had flown away to be happy forever, but that was not possible for her and Nikolai.

In the box, she placed the latest note from him, along with all the others he had written her. And then she carefully set the white feather on the top.

At the airport, the two officials turned Nikolai over to two burly looking CIA officials. Agent Bolton and Agent Driscoll would be his new handlers. Agent Bolton, a portly man, sported a thin black mustache and accented his three-piece navy blue suit with a black fedora. He pushed Nikolai, face forward, toward the wall and frisked him for any concealed weapons. Then he hustled him across the tarmac followed by Agent Driscoll, whose muscular build, square jaw, and blond crew cut gave him the appearance of a navy SEAL even though he wore a three-piece suit. Both men stood aside as Nikolai climbed the stairs and ducked into a private government plane. They followed, directing him to a seat, then sat in the row next to him.

Nikolai leaned his head back against the seat as the airplane taxied along the runway, getting ready for takeoff. Resigned to his fate, his thoughts revolved around Beth and the time they had spent together. During the long flight, he sometimes dozed, and she came to him in tempestuous dreams, her ash blonde hair splayed across his shoulder, her lips pressed against his neck as they rolled wildly in satin sheets, their naked bodies clinging together, desperately trying to become one.

He jolted awake as the plane made a rough landing. With Agent Bolton in front of him and Agent Driscoll behind him, they exited the plane. Once inside the airport, Nikolai noticed that the signs and names of kiosks were not in Russian but in Polish. He turned to Agent Bolton, who led him by the arm. "What are we doing here? I thought I was going back to Russia?"

"We've had a slight change of plans. Our superiors have agreed with your lawyer and decided to give you a little time to think over your decision."

Agent Driscoll added, "We know what a hot-shot scientist you are, but we're only gonna give you so much rope, so don't hang yourself. It would be a shame to have you sent to Siberia."

Nikolai walked out into the chill of the rainy night, flanked by his handlers. Sirens blared nearby as cars whizzed past, sending up a spray of water. Agent Bolton pushed Nikolai ahead of him toward a small car and opened the back door. Nikolai got in, and he followed.

Driscoll got into the front with the driver and turned toward Nikolai. "We've set you up in a small room where you'll be watched. But you will have to work for us, translating and decoding certain transmissions from Russian into English during the short time you have to make your decision."

Nikolai's immense relief left him shaky. He ran an unsteady hand through his hair.

The other agent laughed. "Yeah, and if we have to send you back to Russia, it's not that far."

Nikolai looked out the window as they passed city block after city block of nondescript brown and gray buildings—the only color, the garish reflections of headlights and traffic lights that blazed across the shiny wet streets.

A working class city, he thought. But, no matter. For the moment, he was not in Russia, being hustled on a train for the long ride to a Siberian prison camp.

And maybe, if he studied the situation, he could find a way out. He had tricked the KGB. Maybe he could do the same to the CIA. He would probably never see Beth again unless he could get the false papers he needed to get into the U.S., but here in Poland he could blend into the general population.

Agent Bolton spoke. "The room we have for you is small, and the job is extremely tedious, but this will give you a chance to think about the life you gave up in the U.S. Things would be a lot better if you would consent to work on our weapons project. Our government would be very grateful. And, you might get a chance to see that pretty little wife of yours again. Maybe you could have a second chance to work things out."

The car pulled over in front of a rundown building constructed of concrete blocks. It was surrounded by a high chain-link fence that trapped blowing papers and plastic bags. Nikolai stepped out onto the crumbling sidewalk and was led into the building. Inside the entrance, he noticed a long hall of painted concrete with many doors on both sides and to the left, a concrete staircase with a metal railing that led to the second floor.

Bolton motioned to the stairs. At the top, was another hallway. Agent Driscoll walked to a door marked 14B and opened it with a key. The room was dingy and dark. The walls, furniture, and curtains all seemed to be various shades of brown. The one small lamp dimly lit the place.

Nikolai looked around the dreary room with a hot plate for cooking, unpainted planks for shelving, and a tiny rust-spotted refrigerator. Against the wall, a narrow bed covered with a gray wool blanket brought back depressing memories of his first room behind the diner.

"This is where you'll stay," Agent Bolton said. He pushed another door open. "The bathroom is in here."

Nikolai peered into the concrete block room with a small sink, a toilet and an open shower with a drain in the floor.

Driscoll laughed. "After a month in this rat trap, you might be willing to do just about anything to get out of here. Of course, it looks like a palace next to a Siberian prison camp."

"Well, what do you think?" Agent Bolton asked.

"I will stay here."

"Okay, for now," said his partner, snapping a homing device on Nikolai's wrist. "There are a few Russians who would love to get their hands on you. You made them look very silly, and they don't tend to forget a thing like that."

Agent Bolton pushed back his black fedora. "We have one of our men set up in the next room. He will monitor you and drive you to headquarters for work."

Tipping his hat, Agent Bolton said, "Remember, you don't have a lot of time to make your decision." He and his partner left the room, locking the door behind them. Nikolai heard them knock on the next door, which opened quickly. There was a brief conversation, then the scuffling sound of the two men going down the stairs.

Nikolai surveyed the dismal room again. Sighing, he unpacked his belongings. He put his radio and CDs on one plank shelf and his leather bound books by James Fenimore Cooper on another.

Then, on a rough table by the bed, he placed the picture of his parents, the picture of Amalia with her handkerchief beneath it, and a picture of Beth that was taken at Christmas. Around her picture, he draped one of her silk scarves, which exuded the sweet musky scent of her. He had taken it out of the hall closet to keep as a remembrance of her.

Nikolai lay on the bed and covered his eyes with the back of his hand. He thought of Beth. He remembered their nights of tender lovemaking and her breathless moans of pleasure as they moved in each other's arms. Entrenched in grief, hot tears stung his eyes.

All night Nikolai wrestled with sleep, dozing and waking to this depressing scenario over and over again.

In the morning, he lay awake, listening to sounds from outside. He remembered waking up in Beth's house: the smell of coffee, the comfortable relationship that had developed between the two of them, dinners in her mother's room and of course the ecstatic love they shared.

Nikolai rolled off the bed and circled the room. He would not stay here, and he would not go to a Siberian prison camp. Checking the windows, he found wrought iron bars on the outside. He placed a hand against the wall, smoothing it from corner to corner. There was a heating vent high on the wall. He quietly lifted a chair and placed it just under the vent. Standing on the chair, he found that it was too narrow for his body to fit through.

As Nikolai placed the chair back at the table, he could hear the scuffling from the next room. He sat on the bed with his head in his hands. There was no getting out of this room unless he had a key, and even with the key, he had this homing device that would be very difficult to remove. He would have to come up with something.

At 7:00 the next morning, the agent unlocked Nikolai's door and peered in. Dressed in an army uniform, he motioned for Nikolai to get up. "Come on, Buddy, it's time to go to work."

Nikolai carried his clothes along with the thin towel he had found in the room into the bathroom. He set his razor and shaving cream on the rusty porcelain sink and placed the clothes on the lid of the battered toilet, hoping they would not get wet since there was no enclosure for the shower.

Tepid water, brown at first, spurted from the showerhead near the ceiling. Nikolai leaned his palms against the concrete block wall and hung his head as the lukewarm water ran down his body. His thoughts carried him back to the bright yellow tiles, steaming hot water, and plush towels he had encountered when he first showered in his private bath at Beth's house. Turning off the water, he reached for the thin towel hanging on a hook and thought, *Those in Siberian prison camps would probably consider this a lavish bath.*

After he had dressed, he walked back into the bedroom. A few minutes later, the man appeared at the door and hustled him out of the building. The sky was overcast, but the rain had stopped. They got into a tiny black car and wove through the busy morning traffic until they came to what appeared to be a brownish brick office building about four stories high that was identical to those around it.

However, once inside, the place bustled with action. It seemed to be some sort of central command. All the blinds on the windows were tightly shut. Huge maps of continents covered the walls: desks, each with a computer and other sophisticated eavesdropping equipment, lined the walls and made a path up the center of the room.

People sat at computers or milled around talking to each other, some in English and others in Polish or Russian while phones rang incessantly in the background.

Nikolai was led to a desk in a cubicle in the far corner of the room and was fitted with headphones. After he was given instructions, he sat for long hours, translating and decoding Russian messages that came in. Although his full concentration was necessary because of static noise and communications that cut out, Beth was always in the back of his mind. He wondered what else he could have done to try to convince her of his love.

When he was taken back to his room after the long day's work, the agent in the next room provided him with a meal of beef stew with thick black bread. Afterward, confined to his room, Nikolai was left to his own devices—*almost like solitary confinement,* he thought. Although he wasn't being treated badly, the monotony of the situation and the isolation wore on his nerves, so he took one of *The Leatherstocking Tales* off the shelf.

As Nikolai opened the cover, he looked at Beth's picture, which he had placed there. How he missed not being with her. He wondered if her professor friend, realizing Nikolai's absence, had tried to win her affections. His heart tightened at the thought. He tossed the book aside and jumped off the bed, pacing. He was a trapped animal and there was no way he could get to her.

For all he knew, she might have filed for divorce. She certainly could get one on grounds of desertion. He lit a cigarette and walked over to the window, leaning a hand against the grimy frame. As he looked down into the dark street, he thought, *In reality, who had been deserted?*

19

What Beth was feeling was clinical depression, and she knew it. *Hell,* she thought, *who wouldn't feel depressed in my place.* In the past six months she had not only lost her mother, but she had also lost the love of her life.

When she called Dr. Berton, he agreed that her layman's diagnosis was plausible but insisted she come into the office for a complete physical before he prescribed anything.

As she sat on the doctor's table in a stiff paper gown that tied in the back, Beth studied the mottled green wallpaper and wondered which of the myriad "happy pills" Dr. Berton might prescribe for her. He came in, looking through her file and turned to her. "So, you're not quite feeling up to par."

"I think I'm depressed. I seem to be always down in the dumps."

"Well, this is a natural reaction after losing a parent, but let's take a look and see if anything else is going on." He checked her throat, ears, and glands. As he listened to her lungs and heart, he smiled. "Everything sounds good. Now, just lie back on the table."

As he checked her breasts, she noticed his expression change to a frown. He stopped for a moment and leafed through her file. "When was your last mammogram?"

"Oh, I don't know, maybe a year and a half ago."

"Do you check your breasts on a regular basis?"

"No, I don't. Is there a problem?"

"Well, I feel a mass along the outer left side." He placed her hand on the area so she could feel it. There was something there, and it was fairly good-sized.

"What is it?" she asked.

"I really don't know, but it will have to be removed. I'll make the appointment with surgery. Don't worry. Often these things turn out to be nothing."

Yeah, she thought, *but what if it turned out to be something?*

Sitting at her kitchen table, her mind raced. If the mass was cancerous and the breast had to be removed, she might not be able to nurse any children she might have. She remembered Nikolai's words concerning a woman's body. He had said that the primary purpose was to yield her body to a man she loved, bear his children, and nurture them at her breast.

She realized now, that for her, his words were true. If she died without having had the love of a man or without bearing children, her life would have been unfulfilled.

Beth went into Nikolai's room. In his bathroom, she removed her clothes. Stepping into the shower, she let the steaming water engulf her as she hugged her arms around her body and let her mind wander, conjuring up visions of Nikolai. She dried herself, and even though it was a warm spring evening, she put on her flannel nightgown and a fleece robe. She felt cold—cold to the bone.

As she sat in the semi-darkness of her mother's room, she pulled the hand-knitted afghan around her shoulders, and for the first time noticed the beautiful pattern set in neat squares.

From the rocking chair, Beth could see her mother's perennial garden. The yellow daffodils, pink bleeding hearts and white woodruff created a scene of timeless serenity. Her mother had left beauty everywhere. The words of a country song came to mind, "It's not what you take with you, but what you leave behind when you go." Nikolai believed this, and, oh, how she missed him.

Suddenly, she felt the need to contact him. She hadn't seen him at the university in the last two weeks, nor had he left her any notes. She decided to ask around for his phone number. She just wanted to hear his voice, knowing that that alone would make her feel better.

The next morning at school, Beth ran into Amy Ressler.

"Hi," Beth said. "Hey, have you seen Nikolai around lately?"

"No, he's gone, and it's all very mysterious."

"Where is he?" Beth asked, feeling anxious.

"No one knows. He sort of just disappeared."

"Well, I need to find him. I have to talk to him about something important."

"Well, good luck. I suppose you could try Dean Avery. He might know something."

"I will. Thanks a lot," replied Beth.

Beth made an appointment with the dean for that afternoon. When she entered the room, he smiled and motioned for her to sit. "What can I do for you, Beth?"

Beth sat opposite him, perched on the edge of her chair and sighed deeply. "Dean Avery, I need to speak to Nikolai."

Dean Avery's expression became serious. "I would say that is impossible."

Beth leaned forward. "Has he left the university? Was immigration involved?"

"Officials were here, yes."

Beth faltered. "Oh my God, did they deport him?"

Dean Avery stood. "All I can tell you is that he is no longer employed by the school."

Gathering her strength, Beth stood, too. "Legally, I am still his wife. I think you could at least tell me where he has gone."

"He was the one who refused to involve you in his predicament. We begged him, but he was adamant. Honestly, I don't know where he is. You'll have to go to someone higher up than I for that information."

"What is this . . . top secret?" she asked.

"Just about," answered the dean, nodding solemnly.

At home, Beth sat in her library and quickly leafed through her Rolodex, looking for the number of Nikolai's cousin, Tania.

When the woman answered the phone, Beth's tone was urgent. "Tania, I need to get a hold of Nikolai right away."

"He is not here," she answered in a frightened voice.

"Where is he?"

"Please, Miss, I do not know."

"Tania, I know if he could contact anyone, it would be you."

"I cannot speak about this on the telephone."

"Can I meet you somewhere?" Beth pleaded.

"I will come to your house tomorrow."

The following afternoon, Beth ushered Tania into her living room. The young woman sat, wringing her hands nervously.

Beth leaned forward in her chair and intently studied the young woman who sat across from her. "Tania, where is Nikolai?"

"I do not know," she said, staring at Beth with wide eyes.

Beth thought, *Time to take off the gloves.* "Tania, Nikolai told me you and your husband are in this country illegally," she lied.

Tania jolted forward in her chair. "Oh, no, Miss, that is not so."

"I know it is, and I don't want to call Immigration, but I will if you don't tell me where Nikolai is."

Tania covered her face with her hands and in a tearful whisper, she said, "He has been deported."

"Oh, my God, no! It's all my fault. If I hadn't been so stubborn, he'd be here, not in some Siberian prison camp," Beth wailed.

Tania looked more frightened than ever. "Please, Miss, they did not send him to Russia."

Beth leaped off her chair and grabbed the woman's arms. "Where did they send him?"

"I do not know. I only know that he is not in the U.S."

"Tania, I love him very much, and I believe he loves me."

"Yes, he loves you."

"All right then, you know I would never hurt him. I want to help him and bring him back here. Please, help me do that."

The woman bit her lip.

"Tell me, how can I get in touch with him?"

Tania began to cry. She wiped her eyes with her handkerchief and spoke quietly. "They allowed him one call. He could not tell me where he was but said he was safe for now. But this must be kept secret."

Beth moaned. "Why didn't he come to me when they were deporting him?"

Tania wiped her eyes. "He is a proud man."

After the woman left, Beth thought of Nikolai and was frantic, wondering what to do next. He had said that pride was a sin, and this was where their pride had gotten them.

In her study, she rifled through her Rolodex, looking for the number of her lawyer. The receptionist answered on the third ring.

Beth breathed into the phone, "Bonnie, it's Beth Winters. I need to speak to Jim immediately. It's an emergency."

"Surely, I'll put you right through."

The attorney's anxious voice came through the phone. "What's going on, Beth?"

Beth sighed. "Jim, do you remember a few months ago I asked you about an illegal immigrant and how we could make him legal?"

"Yes, I do."

"Well, it turns out he's this important astrophysicist who fled Russia for political reasons. Anyway, things got complicated, and I ended up marrying him, so he could go back to Russia and return to the U.S. safely."

She heard the attorney's audible sigh but continued. "We really cared for each other, but you know how I am. I was skeptical about his real feelings because it was the only way he could get citizenship. So, we ended up separating. This worked out for a while, but I just found out he was picked up by immigration and deported."

"So, he's back in Russia?" The lawyer asked.

"Well, no, it seems that they've deported him to another country. But, Jim, if he goes back to Russia, they'll send him to a Siberian prison camp."

"I see. So, what do you want me to do?"

"I love him, Jim, and I want him back here as my husband."

"You're still legally married?"

"Yes."

"We'll have to bring in the big guns for this one, Beth, but don't despair. I'll get right on it."

"Oh, one last thing. They picked him up at Fairfield University, where he was working, and I think Dean Avery knows more than he's telling me."

"Okay, that's a good start."

Beth held the phone tightly. "Jim, I can't express how urgent this is."

"I understand, Beth. I'll get right on it."

Her voice cracked as she said, "Thank you."

She sighed. How different things might be if she had just trusted Nikolai's love.

20

On Friday morning, Beth dressed in jeans and a comfortable, oversized sweater. She packed a small bag with a novel and a few magazines for her outpatient stay at the hospital.

In her bedroom, she pulled open the top drawer to her bureau that held her jewelry and picked out a watch. As she put it on her wrist, she noticed the fancy trinket box Nikolai had given her for Christmas.

Beth reverently ran her hand over the painted scene on the top, which showed a young girl sitting on the back of the white Phoenix bird that would magically change into her lover. The two were flying away to live happily ever after.

Opening it, she saw the white feather that had been inside the box when Nikolai gave it to her. She smoothed its silky softness with her finger and remembered that, according to the story, when the girl dropped the white feather, it turned into her lover. She sighed. *If only I could make Nikolai materialize.*

As Doreen pulled into the driveway at precisely 8:15, Beth grabbed her purse and bag and locked the front door behind her. Slipping into the front seat, she sighed, giving Doreen a half-hearted smile. "Thanks for driving me."

Doreen smiled back. "Of course I was going to take you. What are friends for anyway?"

Beth bit her lip. "I just hope everything turns out all right."

Backing out of the driveway, Doreen said, "You're going to be fine."

Their drive to the surgical center was quiet. When Doreen pulled up to the front door, she turned toward Beth and placed her arm over the top of the seat. "You're sure you don't want me to stay while they're doing the procedure?"

"Absolutely not. Go shopping. Just pick me up in about two hours. The doctor said I should be ready to go home by then." Beth opened the door and then turned back to Doreen. "And thanks again.

Beth sat flipping through magazines in the hospital waiting room as she checked her watch. Finally, a nurse came out and called her name. The matronly woman in a checkered smock and hospital-green pants led her to a changing area where she was to remove all her clothes except her panties and put on a hospital gown and paper slippers.

Shivering in the thin gown, Beth sat on a low bench attached to the wall to put on the slippers. The nurse returned and took her to a large sterile looking room with various pieces of medical equipment and an operating table—all in a low-light setting. As the nurses moved around her with robotic precision, manipulating the cold sterile equipment, Beth never felt lonelier in her life.

Beth winced as one nurse stuck an IV needle in her arm while another unfastened the gown and washed the area where the surgery was to be performed with an antiseptic solution. The anesthetic flowing into Beth's arm from the IV made her more and more drowsy. The room loomed far away. Just before unconsciousness claimed her, she pictured Nikolai, with those translucent golden-green eyes smiling down at her, and she breathed the words, "Nikolai, my love."

As Beth slowly regained consciousness in the recovery room, her eyes focused on the face of the nurse standing over her. "My breast—did they have to remove it?" she stammered.

"No, they just removed the mass," the nurse answered.

"Was it cancer?"

"The doctor will be able to tell you, and he'll be in to see you soon."

Beth lay in her bed contemplating what her life would be like if she actually had cancer. She had watched the disease slowly take her mother's strength and vitality and reduce the older woman to a helpless invalid before death finally claimed her.

But at that time, Nikolai had been there to lean on. Beth knew that she loved him and wanted him at her side no matter what her condition. But if she did have cancer, should she contact him?

He might think she was just using him to help her get through a difficult time. He had every right not to believe her. After all, she had not believed him when he swore he loved her.

He had begged her to live in the present moment and not worry about the future, but she could not see her way to that kind of thinking. She wondered what kind of life they would have been living if they had stayed together.

Maybe she would have been pregnant, but in any case, she knew he would have been here with her through all of this. So, how did she ultimately protect herself by sending him away?

She remembered their nights of splendor in Russia. He would make love to her when they went to bed, and often he would wake her in the middle of the night when his rapacious desire for her rose again. If he really didn't love her, why had he been so desperate for her? He didn't have to repeat his amorous lovemaking to convince her that his feelings were genuine. Or was he the kind of man who just couldn't get enough sex?

Whatever the truth, she knew she loved him, and if he were standing here right now—pride or no pride—she would tell him. Suddenly, she understood the supreme importance of his words, “the blessed now.”

The doctor pushed open the door, bringing her out of her reverie. Beth studied his expression, hoping to find a clue to what he might say. He smiled. “We were lucky—no cancer.”

Beth sighed a deep breath. “Thank God.”

“I do suggest, however, that you come in for a mammogram every six months for a while so we can monitor you more closely. The procedure went well, but you’ll have a scar on the outer edge of your breast. In time, that should fade. You can go home as soon as you feel up to it.”

Beth was sitting fully dressed in a rocking chair when she saw Doreen walking toward her. Smiling broadly, she gave her friend the thumbs up sign.

“Doreen wrapped an arm around her and said, “I told you it would be okay.”

Reaching for her purse and bag, Beth said, “I’m just glad it’s over.”

Doreen took her arm. “Let’s get you home.”

As Doreen pulled into Beth’s driveway, she asked “Are you sure you don’t want me to stay overnight with you?”

“No, I’m fine.”

“Well, I’ll call you about nine o’clock to see how you’re doing.”

Beth leaned over and gave her a hug. “Thanks again.”

Beth unlocked the door and went into the kitchen. She put the kettle on to boil and sat in a chair. With a clean bill of health, she could begin to set her plan in motion.

21

As Nikolai padded barefoot around his room in jeans and an unbuttoned flannel shirt, he heard a key turn in the lock. He stubbed his cigarette out in an ashtray on the table but didn't move toward the door.

Why would someone unlock the door? It was Sunday, so he wouldn't be taken to work. He ran a hand through his hair. Maybe the time was up for him to make a decision, and they were ready to turn him over to the Russians. Leaning a hand on the table, he steadied himself. Then, there came a knock at the door.

"Who is there?" he asked in Polish. When he received no answer, he moved cautiously toward the door. That was when he noticed the white feather sliding into the room from beneath it.

With growing curiosity, he bent to pick up the feather and studied it. Then, he pulled open the door. In the hall, looking pale and a little thinner was Beth Winters.

Nikolai stood transfixed. He didn't go to her because he knew that once he held her in his arms, he would not be able to control the wild rush of desire that now throbbed in his temples and coursed through his body.

He simply said, "How did you find me?"

"I talked to your cousin. Then, my lawyer contacted the agents that picked you up and told them I wanted to see you."

"And they agreed?"

"Yes, but they didn't like it, especially when I insisted we were still married."

Nikolai sighed. *So, she hadn't divorced him.*

"As your wife, I insisted on seeing you immediately. Once they agreed, I asked them to keep it a secret. They're good at that, you know."

His expression softened.

"Are you alone?" she asked, glancing past him.

"Of course. Who would I have here?"

"Another woman?" she asked in a mischievous voice. Smiling, he raised one eyebrow. "But I am a married man."

"Haven't you ever heard the word polygamy?"

His smile broadened as he recognized the word. Desperately, he wanted to go to her, but still he held back.

"Can I come in?" Beth asked.

"Of course," he replied, as his eyes searched the hall. The guard must have returned to his room. Nikolai shut the door and extended an arm. "Unfortunately, it is very small and bare."

Beth walked around the room. "It looks fine to me."

Seeing her for the first time in full light, he spoke with concern. "You look thin. Are you well?"

Her eyes misted. "I'm okay now, but I had an operation."

"Where?" he asked.

She touched the side of her breast and said softly, "Here."

Moving close to her, he fingered the top button of her blouse and slowly unbuttoned it, and then the next, and the next until the blouse gaped open. Nikolai pushed it to the side, revealing the scar that snaked along the side of her pale, white breast. Then ever so slowly, his lips moved to that place. Following the line of the scar, he tenderly kissed her there. His arms came around her, gently at first, and then with intense passion that filled him until he felt his heart might burst.

Beth voiced a sob of joy. Gently holding his head to her breast, she whispered, "You were right about everything. When I thought I might have cancer like my mother, your words came back to me over and over again. I feared I would die without the love of a man or without ever having had a child. And I promised myself that after the procedure, I would find you and do my best to make things right between us."

Burying his face in the hollow of her neck, he said, "Everything is right as long as you love me. I wanted to die when I could not have you anymore. That is why I did not care if they sent me to a Siberian prison camp."

Tearfully, she said, "But, Nikolai, I told you to get in touch with me if there was a problem."

"I would never do that. Even if it meant my death, I would never have you think I only wanted you so that I would not have to go back."

"I was such a fool. When I think of the terrible consequences that might have happened because of my stubbornness, it makes me sick," Beth answered, lowering her head.

Kissing her ear, her temple, her neck, he breathed, "This had to be, in order for you to trust my love."

"You're right. I had to experience all of this. I had to learn the meaning of trust and what my true fulfillment as a woman was."

As he pulled her closer, she looked up into his eyes and said, "I owe you so much, and I plan to spend the rest of my life repaying that debt."

He moved his hands on her back beneath the blouse and whispered, "All I want is your love."

Beth moaned, kissing his brow, his rough cheek and his neck.

"Come . . . lie down with me, Beth. Let me make love to you," he murmured.

She sighed. "Yes, my love, now and always."

"*Vsegda*—always" was his only reply.

ACKNOWLEDGMENTS

Albin, Michael. *Henri Troyat Pushkin.* Paris, 1946. Translated as *Pushkin* by Nancy Amphoux, Doubleday & Co., Inc., 1970

Almedingen, E.M. *Russian Folk and Fairy Tales.* G.P. Putnams Sons, 1957

Dostoevsky, Fyodor. *The House of the Dead.* 1861

Feinstein, Elaine. *Pushkin: A Biography*. Ecco (HarperCollins), 1998

Pais, Abraham. *Subtle is the Lord: The Science and Life of Albert Einstein.* Oxford University Press, 2005

Tsvetaeva, Marina. *A Captive Spirit Selected Prose.* Ardis, 1980

Maryl Damian has been an educator at a local college for many years. During that time, she has pursued her dream of writing a novel. *Nikolai my love* is the product of that dream. She lives in Connecticut with her family and devotes many hours to her grandchildren.

CPSIA information can be obtained at www.ICGtesting.com
Printed in the USA
LVOW10s2330250716

497704LV00043B/1104/P

9 781523 377275